"I thought you might be hungry," Logan said. "And…I was feeling bad that you got wet. Again."

As if Ella needed reminding of when he'd found her, soaked to the skin, unable to get into her new apartment. Or being in his apartment, using his towel to dry her hair. Or, most of all, discovering that she was attracted to him more than she had ever been attracted to anyone when she'd first met them, in fact. But maybe the reminder was why she was feeling it so strongly again right now. Enough to make her skin tingle right down to her toes.

"Do you fancy some Thai takeout?" Logan's smile was an invitation all by itself.

Ella's toes were curling inside those fluffy socks as she took a deep, appreciative sniff. "That smells *so* good."

Logan's voice—and smile—were trailing away and his eyebrows were rising. Ella couldn't miss the way he deliberately shifted his gaze after it had drifted down to take in her attire. Or lack of it? Had he guessed she wasn't wearing any underwear at all?

Dear Reader,

After my home country of New Zealand, I think my next favorite place to set a story is in Scotland.

I was lucky enough to live in Glasgow for two years. It might be a long time ago, but the memories have never faded and using it as a setting means I get to rediscover everything I love about the country— the traditions, the stunning countryside with the highlands and the lakes and the beaches, the lovely old stone buildings in the cities and, of course, the people. If I want a passionate but brooding hero, I can't go wrong with a Scotsman, and Logan was a delight to meet. I totally understand why Ella falls in love with him.

As for the medical specialty setting, obstetrics has to be another firm favorite. It has everything— life-and-death emergencies, adorable babies and, oh, the emotion! I have to confess, I can shed a tear when I'm writing these scenes because I'm so there.

I hope you will be, too.

Happy reading!

With love,

Alison xxx

FLING WITH THE DOC NEXT DOOR

———

ALISON ROBERTS

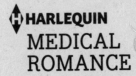

HARLEQUIN
MEDICAL
ROMANCE

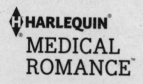

HARLEQUIN®
MEDICAL
ROMANCE™

Recycling programs
for this product may
not exist in your area.

ISBN-13: 978-1-335-73786-1

Fling with the Doc Next Door

Copyright © 2023 by Alison Roberts

All rights reserved. No part of this book may be used or reproduced in
any manner whatsoever without written permission except in the case of
brief quotations embodied in critical articles and reviews.

This is a work of fiction. Names, characters, places and incidents
are either the product of the author's imagination or are used fictitiously.
Any resemblance to actual persons, living or dead, businesses,
companies, events or locales is entirely coincidental.

For questions and comments about the quality of this book,
please contact us at CustomerService@Harlequin.com.

Harlequin Enterprises ULC
22 Adelaide St. West, 41st Floor
Toronto, Ontario M5H 4E3, Canada
www.Harlequin.com

Printed in U.S.A.

Alison Roberts has been lucky enough to live in the south of France for several years recently but is now back in her home country of New Zealand. She is also lucky enough to write for the Harlequin Medical Romance line. A primary school teacher in a former life, she later became a qualified paramedic. She loves to travel and dance, drink champagne, and spend time with her daughter and her friends. Alison Roberts is the author of over one hundred books!

Books by Alison Roberts

Harlequin Medical Romance

Morgan Family Medics

Secret Son to Change His Life
How to Rescue the Heart Doctor

Two Tails Animal Refuge

The Vet's Unexpected Family

Christmas Miracle at the Castle
Miracle Baby, Miracle Family
A Paramedic to Change Her Life
One Weekend in Prague
The Doctor's Christmas Homecoming

Visit the Author Profile page
at Harlequin.com for more titles.

CHAPTER ONE

Being faced with a potentially life-threatening emergency on her first day in a new job, let alone with her very first patient, was not something that Dr Ella Grisham had been anticipating.

She'd been a specialist obstetrician for long enough now, however, to know that the first signs of an emergency could appear at any time. They could also escalate rapidly and, when there were two lives involved, the stakes—and the tension—could reach overwhelming levels surprisingly rapidly.

Ella was quite aware that, in hindsight, she might excuse what was happening for that reason but, right now, the brusque demand from the man who'd burst through the door of this delivery room, after stopping suddenly to stare through the window on the corridor side, was alarming for everyone, including Ella.

Especially Ella?

'What's going on?' He was glaring at her. 'Who are you?'

'Ella Grisham.'

'Ah, right…our new locum. I'm Logan Walsh.'

Ella simply nodded. She had expected to meet the head of department here in the Queen Mother's Maternity Hospital—a separate wing of a large general hospital in Aberdeen—before she actually started her first shift but he'd been away presenting a course in obstetric emergencies the day of her interview last month and was apparently running late this morning due to an urgent administration issue that needed his attention. Nobody had time for introductions, anyway, because a midwife was asking for an urgent consult on a woman in labour.

A woman that Ella was currently still examining. She had the transducer of a portable ultrasound machine in her hand and she turned back to the screen.

'No obvious signs of a placental abruption,' she said.

Judy, the midwife, gave Ella a cautiously

relieved glance but they both knew that even massive internal blood loss could stay hidden for some time. She turned back to the tympanic thermometer she was holding as it beeped. 'Thirty-seven point six,' she reported. 'Heart rate's up to one ten.'

'Blood pressure?'

'One forty over sixty-five.'

'Can someone tell me what's going on, please?' The words were clipped enough to be a command rather than a request. It only took a couple of steps of Logan Walsh's long legs for him to be beside the CTG machine being used for continuous monitoring of both the baby's heart rate and the mother's contractions. He ran the strip of paper, that was long enough to have puddled on the floor, between his fingers.

'Lauren's a thirty-two-year-old primigravida,' Ella told him. 'She's coming up to thirty-seven weeks gestation. No concerns with the pregnancy other than the baby being breech but he seemed to decide it was time to turn around by himself a couple of days ago.'

Lauren leaned back against her pillows, her face almost as pale as the hospital linen. 'It felt like I was being turned inside out,' she put in. 'It was my midwife that told me what had happened and she said it was a good thing because it meant I might not need to have a Caesarean.'

'Lauren came in about half an hour ago with sudden abdominal pain,' Ella continued.

'I checked her,' Judy put in. 'Waters were intact, she wasn't having any contractions and there was no bleeding or dilation on an internal exam.'

'Judy had just called for an urgent consult when I arrived on the ward,' Ella added.

'Why?' Logan's gaze flicked up from the graph paper to land on Judy.

Ella wanted to suggest that it had probably been more than seeing a staff member he didn't recognise that had brought him barging into this room after barely more than a glance through the window. It was more likely to have been an instinct—the same kind that was making the hairs prickle on the back of her own neck. Something wasn't right here.

Judy didn't get the chance to respond to the HoD because Lauren let out a cry. Her husband reached out to put his hand on her forehead.

'What's wrong, babe?'

'That pain's getting worse. It hurts in my shoulders now, too.' She pulled in a sharp breath, and then another, as if it was suddenly becoming difficult to breathe. 'And I think I'm going to be sick.'

Ella had started wiping the gel off Lauren's abdomen at the same time she'd cried out in pain and she had caught her own breath as she felt the rigid muscles beneath the tissues in her hand. She couldn't miss being the sudden focus of Logan's attention either, despite Judy reaching past him with a container in case Lauren was about to vomit. His stare had the intensity of a laser beam.

'Abdomen was soft five minutes ago,' she said quietly. 'And only slightly tender.'

'Blood pressure's dropping.' Judy was watching for the figures to finish appearing. 'Seventy-eight over forty. Heart rate's up to one-forty.'

The blood pressure was suddenly dangerously low and the heart rate too high. Ella didn't need to check the recording being spat out from the CTG to know that the unborn baby was having a deceleration because she could hear the blips of his heartbeat slowing ominously. She picked up the transducer of the ultrasound with one hand and squeezed a new blob of gel onto the stretched skin of Lauren's belly with the other. It took only seconds to find something that hadn't been obvious even a minute or two earlier.

'There's free fluid in the abdomen.' Most likely blood. A lot of it, although Ella didn't pass on either of those thoughts aloud. Logan was the only person who needed to know just how serious this situation had suddenly become.

Lauren was sobbing, between agonised groans.

'Do something,' her husband begged. 'Please…'

'We're going to take Lauren up to Theatre.' Logan's tone was deceptively calm. 'We can get her pain under control there and start giving her some fluids at the same time as getting her ready for surgery.'

'Surgery?'

'It looks like there's some internal bleeding going on,' Ella told him. 'So the sooner we deliver baby, the better.'

'Can I stay with her?'

'We'll see how it goes.' Ella couldn't make promises. In the event of a major surgical emergency you didn't want family members in there watching. 'You can certainly come up as far as Theatre with us. We'll need you to sign the consent forms for a Caesarean section.'

'Are you going to do the operation?'

'No,' Logan said. 'I'll be doing that.'

'You're in the best hands,' Judy assured them as she began opening both doors to the room to allow for the bed to be wheeled through. 'Dr Walsh is our top consultant.'

Ella was blinking at having her first patient whisked from her care like this. Okay, this man was her new boss and maybe he hadn't read her CV and had no idea that she was more than capable of handling an emergency C-section herself but to dismiss her like this, in front of a patient and one of her new colleagues was…well…rather stunningly rude.

She'd probably decide it was mortifying when she gave herself time to think about it and maybe that would be in only a matter of seconds when everybody else had vanished through those doors, leaving her in an empty delivery room.

Lauren was still sobbing as the bed started moving, beside herself now with the fear on top of her pain. 'But I want Ella to look after me…'

'She's coming too,' Logan said, his tone suggesting that it was a given. He turned as he reached the door, his brows lowering as he saw her still standing beside where the bed had been positioned. 'Any time you're ready, Doctor…?'

'Grisham,' Ella muttered as she followed the bed. Not that there had been much point in answering the query. He'd probably forgotten he'd even asked by now. Her HoD was holding onto the rails on one side of the bed, Judy on the other, as they sped towards a lift that another staff member was already holding open for them, the tension of an escalating emergency clearly contagious.

Ella squeezed herself into the small space remaining in the lift as the doors began to close. She found she was still holding her breath as they slid open again a very short time later, giving them access to the theatre suite. She got out to allow room for Lauren's bed to get past and, to her horror, Ella could see a bright red bloodstain beginning to spread on the hospital gown that had become tucked between her legs.

This was definitely the most dramatic start to any job she'd ever had and maybe the worst part was that she was clearly not going to be allowed to take an active role in making sure it didn't become a catastrophe. Ella could only hope that this tall, rugged-looking man who'd simply assumed command—and who, in fact, was the reason she'd chosen to come to this particular hospital in the first place—was every bit as good as his reputation suggested.

At least she knew better than to make idle small talk at an inappropriate time—like when you were scrubbing in for an emergent situation where every second counted.

It seemed that this new locum was every bit as focused as Logan was on the woman they'd just left in the hands of the anaesthetic team to put in a spinal block and the theatre technicians to drape and prep Lauren's skin. A sideways glance as Logan pulled on a hat and tied his mask showed him that Ella was already well into the detailed process of decontamination. She was rinsing off the first soaping by holding her hands up to let the water stream down towards her elbows. He noticed that her nails were short and practical and that she wasn't wearing any rings, although anything other than a plain wedding band had to be removed for surgery anyway. What was far more important was that Ella had just demonstrated skills far more useful than not interrupting his concentration.

'That was good work,' he said gruffly. 'Getting wide bore venous access for fluid resuscitation when someone's that shut down isn't easy.'

'Can the blood bank here do a full group and hold within forty minutes?'

'Of course. And we'll have O negative packed red cells, platelets and plasma here by the time we've run two litres of saline.' Logan used his elbow to dispense the liquid surgical scrub onto his hands and then interlaced his fingers to start a ritual he was so familiar with it was automatic. 'Did you get the chance to do a detailed history?'

'Enough to know she had no red flags for a placental abruption.' Ella had taken the soap-impregnated brush from its sterile packaging and was starting to scrub her nails. 'Her blood pressure's been normal at every antenatal visit, she doesn't smoke and she hasn't experienced any recent traumatic event.'

'What makes you so sure it's a placental abruption?' Logan clasped his arm with his other hand and rotated it as he moved his hand towards his elbow. 'Why wouldn't you think it could be a uterine rupture?'

The glance he got then was wide-eyed. 'Because the chances of that in a primigravida with no history of trauma or surgery are virtually non-existent. What's that saying about thinking of horses when you hear hoofbeats and not zebras?'

'When you're the only maternity hospital for a very large catchment area, maybe it pays to remember there might be a zoo nearby.' It was Logan's turn to reach for the nailbrush.

Ella was unfolding the sterile towel to dry each hand and arm. 'Lauren's not an older mother, she's less than forty weeks gestation with a baby of normal weight.' She picked up the gown on the top of the opened sterile pack, giving it an expert shake before pushing her arms into the sleeves without letting her fingers come through the cuffs. 'As far as anyone knows, she doesn't have a malformed uterus and hasn't got a placenta praevia. She's never had a C-section or surgery for fibroids. She's not even in labour...'

Logan said nothing as he let her finish demonstrating her knowledge of known risk factors for the major complication of a ruptured uterus. While it wouldn't change the initial management of getting both this mother and baby out of danger, it was disappointing that this new colleague was dismissing what was always top of his own list of potential diagnoses with this kind of presentation. He stayed silent as he put on his own gown and gloves. Ella was turning to wrap the tie of her gown around her body while a nurse held the end. She tied it in a bow, clasped both gloved hands in front of her body and stood back, clearly waiting for him to lead the way into Theatre. Her gaze was steady.

'You're quite right,' she said quietly. 'About keeping even the rarest of things in mind.' She didn't let go of his gaze.

Logan was still silent for a heartbeat but then he gave her a single approving nod. 'Let's go and find out, shall we?'

He was right.

Against those unbelievable odds, Logan Walsh had picked the correct cause for the sudden life-threatening deterioration of Lauren's condition. The massive amount of blood that had been lost became dramatically obvious the moment the abdomen was opened and at least a litre of blood spilled out to soak the drapes and trickle onto the floor of the operating theatre.

'Suction, please.' Logan's voice was deceptively calm.

Ella held the tube of the suction unit and could see the collection chamber filling rapidly with another litre of blood. Lauren's husband, sitting on the other side of the screen and holding tight to her hand, couldn't see the operating field but he went several shades paler as he saw the blood on the floor.

It was only when Ella had suctioned even more blood out of the abdomen that the tear in the uterus became evident. For a split second she caught Logan's gaze and it was a silent acknowledgement that, from now on, she would always be more prepared for even the most unlikely diagnosis.

It was impressive just how calmly Logan was dealing with this. Within a remarkably short period of time he was lifting a completely motionless baby from the damaged womb and placing him onto towels that a paediatric registrar was holding. Ella took another glance as the baby was placed on the trolley in front of the senior neonatal paediatrician and a bag mask was fitted over the tiny face to begin an attempt to resuscitate the newborn.

'Is he all right?' The baby's father had

twisted his neck to watch but could see nothing past the backs of so many people.

'Can I see him?' It was Lauren's voice this time. 'Just for a minute?'

'Not just yet.' Logan's voice held a note that Ella hadn't heard before. 'He needs a wee bit of help but he's in the best hands.'

He wasn't just being reassuring without making promises that might not be possible to keep. There was something deeper in that tone. A hint of an empathy that Ella could actually feel rather than hear.

'Suction, thanks.'

This time Logan's tone told Ella not to lose focus on the task ahead of them now—to stop the blood loss and hopefully be able to repair the uterus so that Lauren wouldn't lose the chance to have another child in the future. It didn't look promising with the distortion she could see in the uterine structure but, as the minutes ticked past and more blood products and then whole blood were hung for transfusion, Logan worked with the utmost concentration and a skill that Ella recognised as being possibly the best she'd ever seen to repair the jagged damage.

Even better, the ominous silence from the

corner of the theatre where the paediatric team were working to resuscitate the baby was finally broken by the warbling cry of an infant who sounded as if he'd got over the shock of his tumultuous entrance to the world and he wanted everybody to know he wasn't happy about it.

His parents both burst into tears and Ella could feel herself welling up too, because the survival of a tiny baby against the odds was always going to be something that squeezed her heart hard enough to push a lump into her throat and tears into her eyes, but she had to blink them back. Fast.

How embarrassing would it be if her new boss caught her crying right now? He was already unimpressed that she'd picked the wrong potential cause for a dangerous internal bleed in a pregnant woman. She kept her head down, using the swab she had clasped in some forceps to clear a small pooling of blood, but that wasn't the reason Logan paused his meticulous stitching for a moment. Ella could feel, for that heartbeat, that he was staring at her.

She also had the distinct feeling that he knew just how easy it was for her to get a bit too emotionally involved with her cases. And that he was even less impressed with her because of it.

'I can't thank you enough, Ella.'

But Ella shook her head. 'It's not me that deserves the thanks, Lauren.' She smiled down at the young mother, propped against her pillows, who was holding her sound asleep baby boy in her arms. 'You were lucky enough to be in the hands of one of the best surgeons I've ever worked with—and I've worked with a lot, given that I never stay in one place for long.'

'What made you come to Aberdeen?' Lauren was still too pale and obviously exhausted but happy enough to be smiling back at Ella. 'Can't possibly be for the weather.'

Both women—and the nurse who was tidying Lauren's bedside table—looked towards the window of the room, where the rain was coming down in sheets that would have been thick enough to blur the view of the old grey stone buildings in this older western area of the Scottish city even if the daylight wasn't rapidly fading.

'My grandparents used to live here and I visited frequently as a child. Maybe I felt the need for a place that felt more like home for a change. I've been in California for the last six months, doing some advanced training, and I had a condo right on the beach.'

'Some people have all the luck,' the nurse muttered, but her smile was friendly.

Lauren shook her head sadly. 'You won't want to live on any beach around here.'

'No... And I'm only here for three months, filling in for someone on maternity leave, so it's not worth even looking for my own place.' Ella picked up the chart on the end of Lauren's bed to check the latest vital sign recordings, taking a glance at the catheter bag on the way. Bladder injuries from a uterine rupture were not uncommon and it was reassuring not to see any tinge of pink in the bag. 'I've been given a room in the doctors' residence,' she said when she'd taken in recordings that were all within normal limits. 'Which was another good reason to come here. Not the most important one, of course.'

'What *was* the most important one?' Lauren sounded curious.

'Working with the surgeon who did your operation,' Ella told her. 'He's had some papers published around his mission to reduce the risk of obstetric emergencies, especially in remote areas. He's developed a course to train paramedics and supply refresher courses to GPs and midwives. He also heads a response team that's available to be in the emergency department when a serious case is brought in or they ride out with the crew on ambulances or with helicopter rescue teams if there's enough time. They work with a NETS team as well, which is the neonatal emergency transfer service if an incubator is needed. I'm really hoping I can get involved with the programme while I'm here.'

'You might be out of luck this time...' It was the nurse who was shaking her head now. 'I know people who'd happily give up an eye tooth to get in on that front line obstetric stuff, including the doctor you're filling in for, who's never been included. He's very picky about who gets to work with him, is our Dr Walsh.'

'Hmm...'

Ella's tone was noncommittal but yes... she'd got the impression that her new boss might be rather picky about quite a few things. This morning's emergency hadn't been the time to even think about him on a personal level but those first impressions had been surfacing somewhere in the back of her mind over the course of the rest of the day which had, fortunately, been full of perfectly routine, easy to manage obstetrical tasks, including two straightforward deliveries and an antenatal clinic that had taken up most of the afternoon.

The impression that stood out above all others was the sheer presence of the man. If she'd been a fly on the wall, watching the way he simply assumed command of a situation he'd chosen to walk into, she might have labelled it arrogance but, even though she'd been the person who'd been pushed aside, it hadn't felt as if Logan Walsh was a self-centred or uncaring man. Quite the opposite, really. It was just that what he cared about so fiercely had nothing to do with what others might think of him or the feelings of colleagues he might be trampling on. The intensity of his focus—that, in hindsight, was a perfect match for his very Scottish kind of ruggedness and the dark, slightly unkempt waves of his hair—had been on what actually mattered in the moment, however, and that was saving the lives of this young mother and her first baby.

'It's so good to see you looking so much

better,' Ella said to Lauren. 'You had us all worried there for a little while this morning.'

'I was kind of terrified myself.' Lauren's smile was full of joy now, though, as she gazed at the scrunched-up face of the tiny boy in her arms. 'But he's just perfect, isn't he?'

'He's gorgeous,' Ella agreed. 'But how are you? How's the pain level?'

'The pain's not too bad. I'm just so tired…'

'We had to replace almost your whole blood volume,' Ella said. 'It's only to be expected that you'll feel like you've had the stuffing knocked out of you for a few days but you're doing very well and I can see you're being extremely well looked after.' She smiled at the nurse. 'I'm about to brave that filthy weather out there and find where I'm going to be living because I came straight here from my hotel this morning and left my suitcase at Reception. I don't think I'm far away, though, so if there's any problems overnight I'll be available.'

'The doctors' residence is just across the road from the back of this part of the hospital buildings,' the nurse said. 'But it's Dr Walsh who'll be on call for Lauren. He makes a point of being available for all his own surgical cases.'

Ella blinked. How could any surgeon, let alone a head of department, find the time to do that, on top of running an emergency service for obstetric cases that could be activated at any time of the day or night? Did the man have no life of his own? No need to sleep?

Not that she was about to criticise his lifestyle. Or tread on his toes. She needed some sleep herself after a huge first day on top of the travel and general upheaval that came from shifting her life from one country to another. It would have been sensible to have another night at the hotel with the convenience of the restaurant for an evening meal but it was too late to go back now. Her suitcase— and the keys to her self-contained apartment in the doctors' residence—were waiting for her at the main reception desk.

The weariness, as well as hunger, were even more noticeable by the time Ella had changed out of her scrubs into jeans, sneakers and a warm jumper over her tee shirt. Any thoughts of finding a nearby supermarket were easy to dismiss when all she wanted was to unpack essentials, have a long, hot shower and crash into bed. Passing a vending machine in one of the corridors on the way to Reception, she stopped and selected a ham and salad sandwich in a plastic triangle. At least she'd found an easy way to prevent herself getting any hungrier.

There was no way to stop herself getting very, very wet as she followed the directions they gave her at Reception, dragged her overly large wheelie case across a main road at the first set of traffic lights and looked for an old stone building with a brass plaque above its front door that had the impression of a crown and the grand title of 'The Lodge'.

The mosaic tiling in the foyer was magnificent. So was the ornate ceiling, the chandelier and the sweeping staircase of what must have once been a grand private home. The common areas on the ground floor like the big sitting room to one side seemed to be deserted and Ella's heart sank a little as she realised there was no lift available. She checked the tag attached to the keys she'd been given to both the front door and her own space. Apartment Seven, she confirmed. Second floor.

The big suitcase thumped against every step. Ella stopped to catch her breath on the first-floor landing and then started again, aware that she was still leaving a trail of dripping water from her sodden anorak and the long braid hanging down her back. She was also starting to feel unpleasantly cold.

Apartments Five and Six were the closest to the stairs but the end of the hallway had a wonderful arched window that had the sparkle of lights behind a curtain of the relentless rain so maybe Ella's apartment would have a nice view of the city. It was a huge relief to park her suitcase beside the door with a shiny brass number seven screwed to the dark wood. She fished in her bag for the key and fitted it into the lock.

Or rather she tried to fit it into the lock. She tried both keys. She tried many times but it was quite obvious that there was no way she was going to open this door. She found her phone and tried to call the woman called Jean who'd been so charming when she'd made the arrangements for this accommodation during a phone call from California.

'It'll be perfect for you, Dr Grisham, I promise. You'll find breakfast supplies like tea, coffee and milk, along with all the linen you'll need. The bed will be made up and ready for you and you have my number if there are any problems.'

The response to the number was a message that suggested calling back during business hours on weekdays between nine a.m. and five p.m. As Ella hung up she noticed the warning message of low battery power on the screen of her phone. The option of searching online for a number that would get her through to the hospital's reception desk wasn't looking promising. She was going to have to go out into that horrible weather again, wasn't she?

Ella never normally used swear words but she used one now. Quite loudly. She was tempted to kick the door of Apartment Seven but settled with glaring at it instead. And then she made a growling sound, snatching up her shoulder bag as she turned to head for the staircase again. She hadn't quite finished the turn when the door opposite her own flew open and she froze instantly.

At least she didn't swear again. Out loud, anyway.

This day had started on an undeniably mortifying note when Ella's albeit unknown level of skill had been summarily dismissed in the face of a life-or-death emergency. She'd then offered her senior colleague an inaccurate diagnosis of what was causing that emergency. And now...oh, dear Lord...now, she could almost *feel* him thinking that she was not only demonstrating a lack of control in a frustrating situation but total incompetency in not even being able to unlock a door.

Had she done something terrible in a previous life to earn this kind of karma?

What else could explain this appalling development of discovering that the occupant of Apartment Eight, her closest neighbour, was none other than Logan Walsh?

CHAPTER TWO

IT SHOULDN'T HAVE been so startling to find his new locum standing in the hallway outside his apartment. This was, after all, a residence that was normally used for precisely a situation like this—a locum who was only going to be working at Queen's for a short period. Or the arrival of a new permanent staff member who needed time to find a property to rent or purchase.

Being faced with someone who'd only arrived at his workplace this morning—someone who was going to be working in his own department—made Logan Walsh suddenly realise what it might look like to Ella to find that her HoD was living in what was only intended to be a temporary residence. He could imagine her wondering what sort of consultant doctor, presumably a member of staff who wasn't about to resign, would both work and virtually live in the same building?

But she wasn't looking particularly curious. More like…thoroughly dismayed, with those wide eyes and her lips twisted somewhere halfway between a smile and a scowl. As if he was the last person she'd expected—or wanted—to see right now?

She was also looking like a drowned rat.

A rather angry drowned rat with a dripping tail hanging over her shoulder. Logan could feel an embryonic smile hovering at one corner of his own mouth. He liked that she would choose anger rather than crying if she was in trouble because he'd long ago discovered that it was a far more useful emotion as long as it could be well controlled.

'I…um…heard you,' he said mildly. 'Is there a problem?'

Apart from her being soaked and looking completely exhausted and at the end of her tether? There was more to the way she looked than being either angry or dismayed, he thought. Vulnerable, that was the word for it.

'I can't open my door,' she told him. She sounded as if she was speaking through gritted teeth.

'Shall I try?'

Logan held his hand out for the key without giving Ella a chance to respond and thought he caught a flash of something like a resigned eyeroll before she handed him the key and seemed to find something interesting on the ceiling to stare at. Perhaps it was the decorative plaster rose on the ceiling that provided the anchor for that wonderful antique chandelier he was so familiar with he barely gave it a second glance these days.

The key slid inside the lock easily enough but it wouldn't turn. 'These old doors can be a bit tricky,' Logan said. He rattled the handle and tried again. Then he checked the tag attached to the key ring. 'I think there's been some sort of mix-up,' he suggested.

'Oh…r-really?' Any note of sarcasm was undermined by the way Ella's teeth were starting to chatter so Logan chose to ignore it. He could at least be polite to his new locum. 'You'd better come into my apartment,' he said. 'You can't stand out here in this draughty hallway in the state you're in. I'll ring the concierge and he'll be able to sort it out for you.'

The central heating inside these apartments was efficient and he could see the way Ella closed her eyes in a moment of relief, after dropping her shoulder bag on the floor and starting to remove her soaked anorak. She was wearing a woollen jumper underneath in a golden-brown shade with…good grief… was that a row of llamas across the front of it? Fortunately, Ella didn't notice the direction of his gaze. She was letting her own drift around his apartment as if she was wondering where to put her coat.

'Give it to me,' Logan ordered, grateful for a reason to turn away. There was something about that vaguely childlike oversized jumper that, oddly, had made him curious about the shape of Ella's body beneath in a way that a baggy scrub suit would never do. 'I'll hang it on a chair beside the radiator. There's a stack of clean towels in the bathroom if you want one to dry your hair a wee bit. I'll find the number for Dougal, the concierge.'

He was ending his call as Ella came out of the bathroom, squeezing water from her braid with a towel.

'Dougal's on his way back but he's about fifteen to twenty minutes away, I'm afraid. He actually lives in a small ground-floor apartment, for future reference, but this happens to be the day he takes his elderly mother grocery shopping on the other side of the city. He's very apologetic.'

The band holding the end of Ella's braid had slipped off and the movement of the towel was loosening the tight control of her hair. It was wavy, he noticed as tresses began to break free. As dark as her eyes and it was long enough to be able to cover her breasts if that ridiculous jumper wasn't already doing that job so well.

Logan cleared his throat, a sound that did the trick of stamping on whatever direction his thoughts were trying to go because he had a feeling he was about to get a mental image of Ella riding a horse naked, like Lady Godiva—with her hair protecting at least part of her modesty.

'Apparently the housekeeper who got your apartment ready yesterday pointed out that some of the key tags were unreadable,' he continued hastily. 'So he put new ones on last night and must have put them back on the wrong keys.'

She gave him one of 'those' looks. The ones women were so good at, where they barely moved their eyebrows but could make you feel like a bit of an idiot. It might be a paler version of the glance he'd received when he'd suggested that she might have been given the wrong key in the first place but, added to the way she'd reacted when he'd offered to help, it was impossible not to get the impression that his new colleague didn't find him very likeable.

Not that it mattered. He didn't care what she thought of him personally but it might be awkward to work closely with someone who obviously disliked him.

'Can I get you a cup of tea or coffee? Or a whisky? That might warm you up a bit more quickly.'

'I hate whisky,' she said. 'My grandfather used to reek of it and it put me off for life.'

'Tea, then?'

'No, I'm good. But thank you.'

It was the first time Logan had seen her smile, which was hardly a surprise. The circumstances of their first meeting hadn't exactly been something to smile about, had they? Even that moment of relief in Theatre, when they'd heard the first cry of an infant who clearly intended to survive, hadn't made her smile like this, with that curve of her lips generous enough to crinkle the corners of her eyes. No…she'd quickly avoided looking at him at all in that moment and he'd been relieved that she hadn't been distracted from what they were doing in that complex job of controlling a dangerous amount of blood loss and repairing a ruptured uterus. Thinking back over the hours since then made Logan think he might understand a tension between them that was almost bordering on animosity.

'Your assistance was greatly appreciated this morning,' he told her. 'I enjoyed working with you.'

'Even when I was hearing horses' hooves instead of zebras'?'

Horses' hooves? For a horrible instant Logan wondered if Ella might be telepathic and had caught a fleeting glimpse of that Lady Godiva image. Then he retreated into the comfort zone of the profession that was his life.

'You were quite correct in assuming it was more likely to be a placental abruption from her presentation and lack of risk factors.'

'But it was obvious that she had blood in the peritoneum. And I know that can happen with blood that's backed up through a fallopian tube from a placental abruption, but that's just about as likely as a rupture in an unscarred uterus, isn't it?'

'You reacted quickly and appropriately,' Logan told her. 'And both our mother and baby survived.'

'Lauren tried to thank me when I went to see her this evening but I told her that you were the person she should be thanking. The way you handled a situation that could have easily become catastrophic was very impressive. I can see why you've earned the reputation you've got, Dr Walsh.'

'Logan,' he muttered. The formality felt like some kind of reprimand but he didn't say anything else. Ella had no idea at all of why or how he'd become so good at his job and so capable of managing exactly those kinds of emergencies and he wasn't about to start telling her. Because he didn't want to be reminded of what he'd left behind so many years ago.

He knew the silence had gone on a shade too long by the anxiety he could see surfacing in Ella's eyes at his lack of response on top of the frown of self-recrimination that was already there. He cleared his throat, which had long ago become his go-to method to change the direction of his thoughts and move on.

'You were a pleasure to work with in Theatre,' he said. 'And I don't think I've ever been able to say that to someone on the first occasion I've worked with them. I'm sorry I didn't get a chance to tell you that before now, but I was caught up in some high-level meetings. We're rather desperately hunting funding to extend our ability to keep operating our OERT—the obstetric emergency response team.'

'Oh...'

Logan could see Ella's expression changing like ripples on water from a stone being thrown into a pond. She had the most expressive face he'd ever seen. The anxiety and self-recrimination faded. Any hint of animosity evaporated. Ella was looking interested now. Very interested, with a hopeful undertone.

Interested in *him*...?

It hit him somewhere deep in his gut with the force of...a horse's hoof, maybe? Or was that a zebra, given that Logan didn't remember when he'd last felt a degree of sexual attraction quite like this?

Whatever.

It wasn't welcome. Logan could feel his brows lowering as he tried to think of the best way to make sure this wasn't going to go even a step further.

* * *

Oh, *help*…

What had been shaping up to be a disaster was suddenly an opportunity to talk about what was a part of the main attraction of coming here to the Queen Mother's Maternity Hospital in Aberdeen—the education programme and skilled response team that was becoming a gold standard for managing emergency obstetric interventions both in and out of hospital.

Except that Logan was scowling at her.

But hadn't he just been complimenting her on her management of Lauren's case and the assistance she'd provided in Theatre?

Ella should have been confused. Or intimidated but, to her horror, she could feel a curl of sensation that had absolutely nothing to do with either of those perfectly reasonable reactions.

No… She was looking at this tall, craggy man who was earning an international reputation for being at the top of his field—which also happened to be *her* field—and she was… oh, *God*…attracted to him? Yeah…she recognised that knot of something deep in her gut, that was not unlike excitement or the pleasure of anticipation, currently firing off tingles like microscopic skyrockets in all directions. It was easy enough to ignore, however, because there was something more important to focus on.

Ella swallowed hard as she felt her smile vanishing. 'I didn't say this in my interview because you weren't there, but the real reason I was so keen to take up this locum position is that I would love the chance to get involved with your OERT. It's…' Ella remembered what Lauren's nurse had said about how picky he was about squad members and decided to throw herself on Logan Walsh's mercy. She took a deep breath and smiled at him again—her best smile this time. 'It's a bit of a dream of mine to join one on a semi-permanent basis, to tell you the truth. To be able to use my skills in genuine frontline situations so I could be confident taking up locum positions in more remote areas.'

He didn't smile back.

'You're here for how long? Three months, while Kirsty's on maternity leave?'

'Yes.'

'We struggle for resources to meet our targets for the training days and extra hours for staff members to be on call as it is.' Logan gave a single shake of his head. 'It would be a complete waste to use any of them to train someone who'll disappear as soon as they're remotely familiar with our protocols and setup.'

The disappointment was surprisingly crushing. 'I might stay longer if it's as good as I've heard,' she said quietly. 'I just spent six months in California doing some advanced training in obstetric emergencies and that involved some out of hospital work with an ambulance service.' Disappointment was morphing into something that she didn't need, added to the frustrations the day had already thrown at her. 'You never know,' she went on, a little more sharply than she had intended. 'I could be a resource myself that your team members might appreciate more than you.' Ella picked up her coat and walked towards where she'd left her bag. 'I'll wait for the concierge by my door,' she told Logan. 'He can't be far away now.'

She snatched up her bag but missed one of the handles. Things fell out, including that plastic triangle of sandwiches, a packet of tissues, her phone and a book that had been in there since her plane trip from the States yesterday. It was Logan who picked up the book.

'Are you kidding?'

'What?' Ella had crouched to pick up a slice of hard-boiled egg and some rather wilted lettuce that had fallen out of the salad sandwich to stuff them back into a now dented plastic container. Her intended dinner was no longer even slightly tempting to eat. She'd laugh about this one day, wouldn't she? The final straw in a first day she'd never forget...

Logan was reading the title of her book aloud. *'Architectural Authenticity in the Conversion and Restoration of Historic Buildings.'*

She got to her feet and let her breath out in a sigh. 'I was reading it on my flight yesterday. That subject happens to be my hobby. If I hadn't become a doctor, I would have been an architect.' Her smile felt wry. 'Or maybe I would have just rescued dogs. And ducks.'

Logan was looking at her as if she'd just revealed herself to be an alien from an entirely different planet to his own.

'You wouldn't like to buy an old barn that's ripe for conversion by any chance, would you? One that just happens to have a large duck pond?'

Taken off-guard, Ella let out a huff of laughter. 'Why? Have you got one for sale?'

'As a matter of fact, I have.' Logan waved

a hand to encompass the small sitting room of his apartment. 'The reason I'm living here is because I was stupid enough to buy an old barn a couple of years ago that I haven't found time to even think about converting. My last architect gave up on me months ago after I postponed one too many meetings.'

Ella was staring at him. Wondering if he knew that when he wasn't being completely professional and somewhat surly it took his sexiness to a whole new level?

'I'm only here for three months, remember? It would be a waste of time to get involved.'

'But…' There was a hint of a curve to one side of Logan's mouth that grew into a lopsided smile. 'It might be so good you'll want to stay longer.'

Damn it…

That *smile*…

Ella took the book out of his hands and shoved it back into her bag. 'If you're hitting on me, Dr Walsh, it's doomed to failure, I'm afraid. As tempting as an unconverted barn with its own duck pond might be, I'm not the settling down kind.'

Well, that certainly wiped the smile off his face and, like a punctuation mark, the knock on the door signalled an end to their conversation.

'Dr Walsh?' The voice on the other side of the door was a little muffled. 'It's Dougal here. Is Dr Grisham with you, by any chance?'

'Coming.' Logan went to open the door but the glance he threw over his shoulder had a hint of something that might have been respect in it.

'Good to know,' he said to Ella. 'And don't worry. You're perfectly safe as far as I'm concerned.'

It was the tomato slice that did it.

The one that Logan found beneath the chair he'd used to hang her anorak near the radiator, when he was moving it back to the table. A scrap of food that Ella clearly hadn't seen when she'd been gathering the spilled contents of her bag. Had that sad-looking sandwich been left over from her lunch or was it what she was planning to eat for her dinner?

Not that it was any of Logan's business but he found himself feeling sorry for her.

And guilty about how he'd treated her.

Not when he'd taken over the management of the patient she'd been called to see this morning, mind you. Apart from his personal mission in life to try and ensure that no mother or baby died if medical intervention could prevent the loss, he was the senior consultant on duty and, aside from the glowing reference that had crossed his desk, he had no real idea how competent this new locum was.

No. He was feeling bad about his reaction to her expressing such a fervent desire to be part of the department's emergency response team. He'd seen that hopeful light in her eyes die a rapid death when he'd dismissed any chance of her being allowed to be involved. And she was right. It was very likely, with her experience of different facilities and protocols, that she did have something to offer the team. On top of that, it wasn't easy to find people with the necessary skills willing to take on the disruption to their lives that an extra commitment like being on call for the team represented. So why on earth hadn't he been prepared to even consider it?

Because he was attracted to her and it had caught him so off-guard?

Well, that was his problem, not hers. Ella had made it quite clear that she wasn't interested in being 'hit on' as she'd so succinctly summed it up, so how unfair was it that he was punishing her for how *he* felt?

It was still a niggle in the back of his mind as he ate a microwaved meal for one without even tasting it while he skimmed a recent article on the incidence and management of gastroesophageal reflux disease during pregnancy.

He'd managed to consign what felt like something that needed to be fixed to a mental list of things he would give further thought to in the near future by the time he fell asleep but, weirdly, it was the first thing he thought of when his phone rang at three o'clock in the morning because he knew there was only one reason for that to happen.

Someone in the hospital or the emergency services control room was fielding a call for a potential obstetric emergency and wanted his advice. It would be Logan's call whether the OERT got activated. The conversation was brief but the information received meant that the decision was an easy one. A pregnant woman was in serious trouble and that meant her baby was also in danger.

Logan was well practised in getting himself dressed in the shortest possible amount of time. He usually closed the door of his apartment and then slipped out of the building as quietly as he could to avoid disturbing anyone else who would be getting some probably well-deserved rest but this time, as he shut the door behind him, Logan stopped and stared at the door on the other side of the corridor. He could see Ella's face and the way it had been so alive with the hope that he'd snuffed out.

Two strides and he was tapping on that door.

Just quietly. If she didn't hear him, that was fine. He would still feel as if he'd done the right thing.

But Ella did hear him and she must have woken up instantly to have blinked any traces of sleep from her eyes by the time she opened the door.

'An OERT activation's just come in,' Logan told her. 'ETA of ten minutes to A&E. How fast can you get some clothes on?'

CHAPTER THREE

ELLA HAD BEEN wearing the leggings and a big tee shirt she wore as pyjamas. It took thirty seconds to pull her warm jumper on and jam her feet into her sneakers.

She had to run to keep up with Logan. She might have only had a few hours' sleep but, as she raced down the stairs and out into the night, it felt as if her sneakers had grown a pair of wings. Not that she could keep up a conversation, but she didn't need to. Just an affirmative sound was enough to let Logan know she was taking in the information as they ran along the street and around the corner to the main entrance of the emergency department. Fortunately, the torrential rain of earlier in the evening had stopped for now.

'The paramedic did a course with us not long ago and called this in early while he was still on scene,' Logan relayed. 'Thirty-eight-year-old primigravida, thirty-one weeks gestation with sudden onset preeclampsia symptoms including pulmonary oedema. Oxygen saturation down to eighty-eight percent and blood pressure through the roof.' Logan was starting to sound a little out of breath himself and his pace slowed as his phone started ringing.

His responses were terse and he ended the call swiftly.

'Patient's having a seizure en route,' he told Ella. 'Last blood pressure recording was one ninety over one twenty. ETA four minutes now. Someone from Neonatal Paediatrics is on the way in case we need to deliver.'

They could see the big red sign with a white *H* and *A&E* beneath it beside an arrow pointing towards the entrance. Staff were waiting with packs containing scrub suits and booties to go over their footwear and it seemed like only seconds later that they were heading into the main resuscitation area. Ella tucked her hair under a cap and tied a mask around her face. There were people coming from all directions and the tension in the department shot up as a nurse gave them the latest update from the crew rushing the pregnant woman towards them.

'She's gone into cardiac arrest. CPR under-way. ETA less than two minutes.'

Logan was suddenly centre stage, giving clear and calm directions.

'Start the clock,' he said, and someone pushed the button on a clock that began a time count from when their incoming patient had gone into cardiac arrest.

'We need three resus teams,' he continued. 'One to cover CPR, another one to set up a neonatal resus area and I'll cover the obstetric side of things along with my registrar, Dr Grisham.'

Ella could feel curious gazes on her but only in passing as people swiftly responded to further rapid instructions from Logan.

'CPR protocol to stay the same as normal for both chest compressions and ventilations except that the hand position for compressions is a few centimetres higher on the sternum. Patient to stay supine. You'll need an extra set of hands to provide left uterine deviation. We'll need to set up for a potential resuscitative hysterotomy.'

Ella could hear Logan checking off the equipment that needed to be set up in a sterile area. A scalpel, blunt scissors, clamps, a suction unit, sutures, antiseptic.

'Just a bottle of iodine'll do,' he was saying. 'We might not have time for any other skin prep.'

The neonatal team was on the other side of the resus area, setting up a space that would be used to resuscitate an infant that could well be shocked, with supplies like airways and a tiny bag mask unit, oxygen, umbilical IV access equipment and a baby warmer. A ventilator was being pulled into position at the head of the main bed, along with a defibrillation unit and an IV trolley. The pace was enough to make Ella's head spin but she was more likely to get in the way right now than help find and set things up in an unfamiliar setting. She found herself watching Logan and becoming increasingly impressed with how calm he was and how everybody was following his lead without hesitation. She thought she heard the sound of a siren in the distance and her thoughts went instantly to a pregnant woman heading towards them who was, unknowingly, facing what had probably been unthinkable even a few hours ago—a very real risk of losing both her own life and that of her unborn child.

Resuscitative hysterotomy was the new term for what used to be called a perimortem C-section. Getting ROSC, or return of spontaneous circulation, in a pregnant woman was far more difficult because the uterus compressed veins and arteries and reduced venous return and cardiac output during re-suscitation. That was what the clock was ticking up to. If they didn't achieve ROSC within four to five minutes of the heart having stopped, the decision would need to be made to get the baby out as quickly as possible to improve the chances of survival for both mother and baby. Current research suggested that the time frame could be extended and still achieve good results but the sooner it could happen the better.

Ella saw that the decision had been made the moment the doors of the ambulance bay opened and a stretcher came towards them at speed, with a paramedic still doing his best to keep effective CPR going. She saw Logan glance at the clock, which was now reading three minutes, ten seconds. Twenty seconds by the time the stretcher was in Resus and hands were reaching to transfer the woman to the bed.

'On the count of three... One...two... *three...*'

Emergency department medics were ready

to take over the CPR, with one person doing compressions, pausing for only a matter of seconds to allow the airway physician—an anaesthetist—to intubate her and position the bag mask unit, now attached to the hospital's overhead oxygen supply, over her nose and mouth. A third doctor placed his hands on the side of the woman's huge belly and pushed the baby towards the left to take pressure off major vessels and allow blood to return to the heart. Information was being relayed as rapidly as possible. There had been two cycles of CPR completed en route. Drugs had been administered. Defibrillation had not been successful.

Logan absorbed the handover information but another minute had ticked past and he'd already made the decision. He had a gown over his scrubs and shoved his hands into a fresh pair of gloves.

'Stand back, please, everyone. We're going to do an RH. Ella? Are you ready?'

'Yes.' Ella, also gowned and gloved, stepped up to the side of the table opposite Logan.

A nurse tipped iodine over the stretched bare skin of the woman's belly and Ella heard a gasp from behind her as Logan used the scalpel to make a long incision that opened the abdomen in the midline from the pubic symphysis to the umbilicus. She had the blunt scissors ready to hand him to get through the muscles beneath the skin and then to open the uterus. She held her breath as she watched him feeling for the closest part of the baby he could find through the incision and then getting a firm enough grasp to be able to apply traction.

'Fundal pressure, please, Ella.'

Ella pushed down on the top of the uterus to help Logan pull the baby out. She grabbed the clamps to close off a section of the umbilical cord for Logan to cut through and then held out a towel for him to put the baby on, turning in almost the same instant to hand a totally limp newborn over to the neonatal team, less than sixty seconds from when Logan had made that first incision. They rushed the tiny boy to the resuscitation area they'd set up on the other side of the room and he was lost to view within seconds.

CPR was in progress again on the mother.

'Stand clear,' someone warned. 'Shocking...'

The woman's body jerked but the static on the overhead monitor settled to reveal no change to the ominous wavy line of ventricular fibrillation.

'Still in VF,' Logan stated calmly. 'Ella, draw up a bolus dose of oxytocin, please. I've almost got the placenta now.'

She handed the new bag of saline to a nurse to hang, moments later, with the drug added that would help prevent excessive bleeding from the uterus by causing it to contract.

Logan wanted to control any immediate blood loss as well. 'Let's clamp any actively bleeding vessels here and then we'll pack the abdomen.'

Ella had never tried to operate while chest compressions were ongoing. She handed clamps to Logan and watched the way he carefully timed the moment of trying to clip them onto a bleeding vessel at the point of the pressure on the sternum being lifted. The two minutes before the next shock was due to happen seemed to pass in a blink.

'Stand clear… Shocking…'

And this time, perhaps helped by CPR after the dramatic intervention to remove the baby and relieve the pressure on blood vessels, the mother's heart started beating again. Just a few uneven spikes could be seen initially but then it settled into a more regular rhythm.

The airway doctor had his fingers against the woman's neck. 'I've got a pulse,' he said. 'Just. BP still not recordable and she's not trying to breathe for herself yet.'

'Let's get some sedation and analgesia on board,' Logan directed. 'I don't want her waking up in pain.' He and Ella were packing gauze into the gaping wound on the abdomen, ready to cover it and move their patient. 'Have we got a theatre on standby?'

'Yes. They're ready and waiting.'

'Good. Let's move.'

Ella took a look over her shoulder as they headed to Theatre. She could see the neonatal team still working on the baby that had an endotracheal tube in place with his lungs being inflated by someone holding the miniature bag mask. Someone else was using only two fingers to provide gentle, rapid chest compressions.

It wasn't looking good.

Logan gave Ella the lead role in the surgery they needed to do to repair the aftermath of the resuscitative hysterotomy but he was going to be right there and he wouldn't hesitate to step in if he thought it was necessary.

It was something of a miracle that they'd

got this far with this patient still alive and now they needed to scrub in properly and manage a complicated case on someone whose name they still didn't know. They also had no idea whether this first-time mother had brain damage from lack of oxygen when her heart had stopped functioning, whether she might have suffered a devastating stroke from the uncontrolled blood pressure or could be facing a dangerous infection from a less than ideal operating environment in the emergency department, but Logan liked that Ella was approaching her work with the assumption that everything she did was as important as it would be on an otherwise healthy patient.

'So...' Her glance was direct as they scrubbed in, side by side, as they had for the first case they'd worked on together. Was that really less than twenty-four hours ago? Oddly, it felt like he'd known Ella a lot longer than that already. 'Where do you stand on the double-layer versus single-layer closure for the uterus?'

'Where do *you* stand?' he countered. This was his chance to find out a lot more about Ella professionally. He'd already put a lot of trust in her by bringing her on board for a OERT callout but, he had to admit, he was yet to feel that it might have been an unwise decision. She was calm and competent under a high level of stress and she provided an extra set of hands that almost felt like an extension of his own with her ability to anticipate what was needed.

'I know there's still debate but I think the evidence is leaning towards a double-layer closure improving uterine scar healing and reducing the risk of a scar defect in a future pregnancy. I also know it takes more time.'

'We're hardly under pressure to clear Theatre for the next patient at this time of night.' Logan rinsed the soap off his hands and arms. 'And our patient's stable from a cardiovascular point of view. I'd do a double layer.'

Ella's nod was brisk. She was already thinking in broader terms than the task ahead to close the surgical wounds.

'I'd like to get another of bloods off stat and get a full picture of current liver enzymes and kidney function. And a platelet count. We need to start antihypertensive and anti-convulsant treatment for the eclampsia and what protocol do you have for obstetric post-cardiac arrest here? Do you hand her over to Cardiology?'

'We'll have a full team onto it by the time

we've got her settled into the intensive care unit, including Neurology and Anaesthesia while she's being ventilated.' Logan reached for his sterile towel. 'But first things first. You focus on patching her up.'

Which Ella did. As competently as Logan was already coming to expect from her work. Her sutures were neat and her hands deft as she juggled forceps and a needle holder and demonstrated well-practised movements as she looped and locked the stitches. At some point, as the first blood test results got reported back to the team in Theatre, they heard that the baby was alive and had been transferred to the NICU and they finally learned the name of this young mother.

'Iona McTavish,' Ella repeated. 'That's such a pretty name.'

Something in her tone changed the atmosphere in Theatre. The patient whose body was being meticulously mended by Ella had, a little disconcertingly, just become a real person. A young mother with a tiny baby who was fighting for his life in another part of this hospital.

'And so Scottish,' Ella added. 'I've been to the island of Iona and it has to be one of the most beautiful places in the world, I think.

Do you know there are forty-eight Scottish kings buried there?'

No. Logan didn't know that, and he didn't want to think about anything other than clinical information and that included the threat of a painful tug on his own heartstrings that was hovering ever since the news that Iona's baby was still alive. He knew that keeping a professional distance was key to providing the best care possible for his patients. What he did know and needed to focus on was that Iona McTavish's blood pressure was still too high but improving and there had been no further seizure activity during the surgery. Even better, her heart rhythm had remained stable and they were finally able to meet with her family and tell them that things had gone as well as they could have hoped for so far.

They didn't need to warn the shell-shocked partner, Gregor, or Iona's parents how critical the condition of their loved one still was, however. The bank of monitors around the bed where she was lying so motionless amongst a tangle of tubes and wires, with people adjusting infusions and ventilator settings and recording measurements, made it frighteningly clear that she was still in danger.

'We'll be keeping her in therapeutic hy-

pothermia for another twelve hours or so,'
the intensive care consultant was explaining
to Gregor. 'And we'll keep her sedated and
ventilated until we get everything under control. We won't be able to make any predic-
tions about the extent of any potential brain
damage until we know more. We'll arrange
for an EEG to be done to assess brain activity in the next few days.'

It was Ella who broke the impersonal clinical atmosphere after a whispered conversation with a nurse. She touched Gregor's arm
and Logan caught the glance that was offer-
ing a level of empathy that was as disconcerting as the way she'd talked about Iona
in Theatre.

'You can come back to be with Iona soon,'
she told Gregor softly. 'But would you like to
come and meet your son? We've been told it
would be okay, just for a quick visit.'

Gregor had his hand pressed to his mouth,
struggling with his emotions, and Logan
could see the way Ella drew in a deep breath.
'I could come with you,' she said.

Gregor nodded and it was only then that
Ella's glance caught Logan's. The way she
caught a corner of her bottom lip between
her teeth suggested that she might be worried

she'd overstepped a boundary but he echoed
Gregor's nod. It would be a good thing to
dial down the emotion in this space that Ella
was contributing to more than he would have
liked. He'd get someone to take Iona's parents
to the relatives' room too, and then he would
be able to focus on doing his job to the absolute best of his ability.

The way he always did.

He nodded again.

'Take your time,' he added quietly, stepping
towards Ella as she followed Gregor from the
room. 'And then grab some rest before our
day shift starts, if you can. I'll stay here for
a while.'

He could see that Iona's husband was waiting for Ella to join him in the quiet corridor
that connected each space in this intensive
care unit to the central desk. He needed to
be shown how to get to the neonatal intensive care unit, of course, but there was more
in his glance than waiting for a guide. He'd
bonded with Ella as Iona's doctor, Logan realised. Had it been that moment of palpable
empathy between them, when she'd touched
his arm? Or was it just the way Ella was—
like how she'd instantly made a connection

when she'd learned the name of the patient she was operating on?

She was his complete opposite, Logan realised.

So how on earth had it felt as if they fitted together professionally so well? Was it a case of two sides of the same coin?

Whatever...

Logan turned back to the screens and it might have been deliberate that he was thinking of this patient as their post-cardiac arrest case, rather than by her name, as he focused on the information that multiple monitor screens were providing.

What actually mattered, as far as his new locum was concerned, was that she was competent. So much so that he would be happy to involve her to whatever degree she wanted in the OERT while she was here at Queen's. The intensity of working on this case with her tonight had done more than he could have hoped for. They'd not only been successful against huge odds, but the professional connection between them had strengthened enough to make any personal reaction to this woman irrelevant.

That blip of physical attraction had been dealt with. It would not be a problem again.

* * *

The baby's name was Finlay and Ella fell in love with him the moment she stood beside the incubator when his father was taken in to see him for the first time. The tiny baby looked so vulnerable with nothing on but a disposable nappy that looked far too big and a little woollen beanie that covered his head. He had heart-shaped electrode stickers to monitor his heart on a chest where you could see every rib and tubes and wires everywhere. Big tubes for the ventilator, a smaller nasogastric tube and narrow cannulas that disappeared into the bandage holding a splint onto an arm so tiny it looked like a twig.

Gregor was only allowed a brief visit that first night but Ella took a photograph of him with his face beside Finlay's head on the other side of the plastic barrier so that he could show Iona's parents. And Iona, when she woke up.

If she woke up…

That was another reason that Ella's heart went out to this particular baby who might never know his mother and she found herself heading towards the NICU every chance she got over the next few days. She was there when they took him off the ventilator and watched through the window as the neonatal team removed the invasive tube inside his airway that was attached to the ventilator, replacing it with a CPAP device that covered his nose and supported his own efforts to breathe instead of doing it for him. She stood there for long enough to see that his team were happy with how he settled afterwards and she crossed her fingers, hoping that his mother would be able to start breathing for herself soon as well.

Ella sat beside the incubator for a while, the day after the CPAP was in place, when Gregor was sitting with Iona and that was when she saw Finlay open his eyes for the first time. Just for a few seconds before he drifted back to sleep but it felt like he was looking straight back at her and Ella had to wipe tears from her cheeks, hoping that none of the NICU staff had noticed. It was one thing for a doctor to be interested in following up on a baby they had delivered under circumstances that were still the talk of the hospital but she knew nobody would approve of becoming this emotionally involved.

She didn't approve of it herself. But she

knew she could avoid it affecting her ability to do her job.

And, sometimes, she just couldn't help it.

Logan could see her through the window.

Sitting beside that incubator.

She had a mask and gown on and even a cap over her hair, which should have been quite enough of a disguise, but he knew that it was Ella and not one of the NICU nurses watching over this baby. Weirdly, he could actually *feel* it was Ella but he didn't realise why until he saw her lift her hand to wipe tears from her face and he remembered what he'd seen in that moment they'd heard the first cry of that baby who had been lucky enough to survive being in a uterus that had ruptured. In the split second before Ella dipped her head he'd seen her eyes begin to fill with tears. He'd seen—and felt—the emotional connection she already had with that case.

And, while he couldn't fault her performance so far, it was early days and this intensity of her involvement with a patient was decidedly disturbing. Logan would never, ever allow himself to have that kind of connection with a patient—adult or infant.

With anybody, actually, patient or not...

With good reason, because you couldn't do your job as a doctor to your best ability if you couldn't keep a professional distance from your patients and, on a personal level, he was well aware that out-of-control emotions could influence how you thought or behaved, even if it was subconscious.

Logan had long ago built protective barriers to ensure that he was safe from the kind of danger that could come from losing a professional distance but, for a worrying moment, he wondered if they weren't as strong as he believed them to be. Could something make them crack?

Something like seeing Ella not only wiping tears from her face but smiling at the same time, as if something joyous was happening? A kind of joy that Logan never experienced in his work. A very pleasing sense of satisfaction, of course, or relief that could be quite intense was the closest he got to letting go.

And that was exactly how he liked it to be.

So he was horrified to feel a lump in his throat. Something jagged and unpleasant which, if allowed to get any bigger, might threaten to bring tears to his own eyes. He could feel himself scowling as he pushed back against such an unwelcome ambush but he wasn't quite fast enough and he could feel a shaft of that despair escaping before he could slam a familiar mental door.

That newly qualified doctor who wasn't experienced enough to recognise the danger. The pregnant woman in the emergency department who was in the process of losing her baby and bleeding to death herself because the diagnosis of *her* ruptured uterus was taking too long.

Logan had to physically turn away to shut down what could only be a destructive line of thought. He'd find the neonatal consultant and get her to fill him in on the McTavish baby's progress. He should have simply picked up the phone in the first place and stayed well away from this particular area of the hospital—like he usually did. He didn't turn away quite quickly enough, however. As if she felt him glaring at her, Ella had turned to look at the window and, in that split second before he kept moving, he saw her eyes widen enough to convey that she was startled. Shocked, even?

Not that he was about to let that bother him. Logan was her boss after all and Ella was simply a locum consultant who might be proving herself very good at her job but the jury was still out on whether that emotional involvement with her patients might affect her performance. For everybody's sake, he needed to keep an eye on her, Logan decided.

From a safe distance, of course.

CHAPTER FOUR

As ELLA'S FIRST week anniversary of starting her locum at the Queen Mother's Maternity Hospital rolled around, she was still waiting for another chance to work with Logan Walsh on the obstetric emergency team. Or even in the day-to-day routine of working in a busy obstetric hospital, for that matter.

It almost felt as if he was avoiding her, which would be weird but, on the other hand, the last time Ella had seen him in days was when he'd been glaring at her through the windows of the NICU when she'd been visiting Finlay. Mind you, she'd been incredibly busy with deliveries and surgeries, outpatient clinics and high-risk pregnancy patients who'd been admitted for monitoring. Even a CEO was allowed days off too, although she hadn't seen Logan in the hallways of the doctors' residence either.

And, she had to admit, she'd been keeping her eye out for an encounter and *not* seeing him in the residence or working with him in the hospital was adding a frisson of mystery that was having the effect of making him rather more interesting.

Okay…attractive. But she wasn't going there. Not after that cutting little comment about how safe she was from him hitting on her. Good grief…the man couldn't even take a joke and she'd only been trying to lighten the atmosphere after he'd rejected her request to join his specialist team so bluntly. To get such a curt rejection on personal grounds as well could have made working with Logan Walsh unbearable but he'd more than redeemed himself by inviting her to assist with the resuscitative hysterotomy case, so Ella was quite prepared to forgive his grumpy quirks—including the way he'd been glaring at her in NICU.

She really had nothing to complain about in this new chapter of her life.

Especially today. She'd been in this very delivery room on her first day last week, feeling like the new girl at school and not even that welcome when her management of her first patient here had been overridden so presumptively. But things had only improved from that point and Ella was now loving this new position.

That first patient, Lauren, had been discharged yesterday, after making a good recovery from her complicated delivery with the uterine rupture. Ella had been delighted to hear this morning that Iona McTavish—her even more dramatic case in that first twenty-four hours here, was now making good progress. The high blood pressure that had caused the complications in her pregnancy was finally under control, any seizure activity had stopped and her liver and kidney function was improving. While she still hadn't regained consciousness, and had had a setback with a chest infection, her sedation was being lightened so that she could be carefully weaned off the ventilator. An EEG that had been done had been reassuringly normal and her family were desperately hoping she would wake up without evidence of significant brain damage.

Baby Finlay was proving to be a little champion. When Ella had popped into NICU to see him this morning she found him having some skin-to-skin time with his dad, Gregor, with his adorable little button nose visible for the first time because the CPAP device had

ALISON ROBERTS 75

been removed. Ella was acutely aware that
the family's relief—and cautious joy—in the
survival of Iona's baby was providing, at least
to some degree, a balance for the awful anxiety of their vigil for Finlay's mum. She was
feeling it herself...

Best of all, however, Ella's current patient
was the perfect way to celebrate the end of
her first week at Queen's because it was a
twin birth and multiples were her absolute favourite kind of deliveries. This was a woman
she'd already met at an antenatal clinic this
week, as well, so she was not only now familiar with where everything was in her new
hospital and knew most of her colleagues, she
had had the chance to discuss Melissa's desire
to have as little intervention as possible when
she gave birth to her twin girls. The mother
of two young boys had already agreed to give
up her dream of a home birth in order to have
specialist help and facilities on hand but she
was still hoping to deliver both twins without the need for a C-section, even though one
twin was in a breech position.

The room was getting crowded because
there were two midwives here and extra paediatric staff to cover the newborn checks for
two babies. Ella was already in the room as

the consultant on hand in case the breech position for the second twin led to any complications but, for the moment, she was keeping in the background.

Judy was one of the midwives involved and she was kneeling on the floor, peering up to see what was happening as Melissa squatted beside the bed, being supported by her partner, Hamish, who was rubbing her back and adding to Judy's verbal encouragement and reassurance, but Melissa was groaning so loudly with the pain of the strong contractions she was experiencing it was doubtful she even heard the support.

'The baby's crowning...' Judy told her. 'No...the head's gone back in again. She's playing turtle...'

Melissa's groan got louder and she bent her head as she kept pushing.

'Here she comes... One more big push...'

'Push, Mel,' Hamish chimed in. 'Push, push, *push*...'

Moments later, Judy caught the slippery infant as it emerged and then passed it through Melissa's legs so that she could pick up her baby and hold it to her chest with the umbilical cord still attached.

'Oh...oh...' Melissa was in tears now.

'Look, Hamish…isn't she beautiful? Get your buttons undone on your shirt. You're going to hold her while I push out her sister, remember?'

The second midwife put the bean bag down beside Melissa. 'Are you still okay in this position?' she asked as she helped shift the newborn girl into her father's arms and tuck a blanket over them both. 'Do you need a break? Would you prefer to get on the bed for number two?'

Melissa opened her mouth but couldn't say anything as a new pain hit her. Gasping, she sank down onto her knees and put her hands on the floor as the contraction grew stronger. Ella moved so that she could see what was going on. The waters from the second twin had clearly broken and the legs appeared as the contraction faded. The baby was half out, in a sideways position, and its legs were moving in a cyclic motion.

'Big push with your next contraction, Melissa. Baby's trying to help. You're almost there…'

Ella moved in as she realised the baby wasn't rotating as expected with the next contraction and she knew exactly what was going on.

'Your baby needs a bit of help,' she told Melissa calmly. 'I think one of her arms is trapped and that's stopping her being able to come out. I need to move her a little. Are you okay with that?'

'Yes...' Melissa sounded frightened. 'Please...just help her come out...'

'Do whatever you need to do, Doctor,' Hamish added.

Ella knelt behind Melissa. This was a procedure she had done before, but it needed to go smoothly or the situation could deteriorate rapidly.

'You'll feel my hands going in to hold baby,' she told Melissa as she slipped flat hands onto the baby's torso, her thumb tucked beside her fingers, one in front on the tiny chest and the other behind on the back, her fingertips in far enough to almost touch the unborn head. She gently pushed the baby back into the uterus a little to give her room to manoeuvre. 'And now I'm turning her.'

She rotated the baby forty-five degrees in the direction it was facing, using her bottom hand to sweep the baby's anterior arm across its face and body to release it under the pubic arch.

'There we go…' she said quietly. 'Almost there. You're doing *really* well, Melissa…'

She rotated the baby back, far enough for it to be in the correct position for a normal breech birth and then, with a simple shoulder push, the head was delivered and the baby was born.

Twin number two began crying immediately and Ella could feel a collective sigh of relief coming from everybody in the room. The midwives were helping Melissa to a position where she could hold her second born to her chest, against her skin, and she ended up leaning on the beanbag beside her partner, the baby tucked into her arms, its head almost touching that of its twin in the father's arms.

The medical team backed off for a moment. Ella and the midwives were watching for any undue postpartum bleeding and the imminent arrival of the placenta. The neonatal specialists were keeping a close eye on these babies and it would be time to cut the umbilical cords and give them a thorough check and another Apgar score very soon but, even if it was only for a matter of seconds, this time for a brand-new family to be connected like this and bonding in a wash of pure joy was too precious to take away.

Ella knew she had tears on her cheeks as she watched the parents' heads touching as they both gazed down at their infant girls but she didn't care. Even when she looked up to see that Logan had slipped into this delivery room at some point during the tense moments of delivering the second twin. She was by no means the only person present who didn't have dry eyes right now and that hint of a crooked smile on Logan's face before he turned and left the room again suggested that he was just as happy with the outcome as everyone else, even if he had no intention of showing it.

Ella was quite professional enough to keep things hidden herself. Okay, showing a bit of emotion witnessing the overwhelming joy these parents were experiencing with the arrival of two healthy, beautiful babies was fine. But that knot of sensation Ella was experiencing thanks to seeing not only that hint of a smile on Logan's face but the way he'd caught and held eye contact with her for a heartbeat before he'd left the room was most definitely not something she wanted anybody else to notice.

She was planning to ignore it herself, in fact. She'd been quite confident that she had a lid on that very unexpected—and unwelcome—attraction she'd felt to her new boss when she'd first arrived and...okay, maybe she'd been thinking about him and keeping an eye out for him, but she wasn't thinking about him in *that* way. This fizzing sensation deep in her gut was because of the atmosphere in this room. The miracle of two new lives beginning and the satisfaction of successfully navigating the kind of medical challenge that could make obstetrics a bit of a rollercoaster but also made it one of the more exciting specialties to be part of.

She was happy, that was all it was. The kind of happiness that would have made her do a little dance if she'd been somewhere nobody could see her. But she wasn't alone and she was completely professional so she simply smiled instead.

'The cords have both stopped pulsating now,' she said. 'Are you happy to have them cut now, Melissa?'

Good *grief...*

Logan had turned into the corridor that led to the staffrooms with lockers and showers and changing facilities at the end of a particularly hectic day and the last thing he'd ex-

pected to see was someone ahead of him...
dancing?

Not just someone.

Ella Grisham.

Still in her scrubs and clearly unaware that
anyone was behind her. She had her arms in
the air, her head bobbing and...yes...her feet
were doing a kind of skippy thing. Just for a
few steps and then she straightened her back
and lifted her chin as if she was collecting
herself before she bumped the door of the
locker room open and went inside.

Logan paused long enough to take a steady-
ing breath as he felt surprise morph into a
shaft of sensation that went straight to his
groin. That...sexual attraction. Unwelcome,
because Ella didn't fit into any category of
what he considered to be safe—or possibly even acceptable—liaisons with women.
This was a woman who wore her heart on her
sleeve, for goodness' sake. She got too emotionally involved with her patients and cried
easily. She also wore childish jumpers and
wanted to rescue ducks. Maybe the surprising
thing was that Logan *hadn't* seen her dancing
before this. Or was the biggest surprise that
he couldn't deal with that inappropriate attraction as easily as he would have preferred?

When he emerged from the locker rooms having changed out of his scrubs and saw Ella ahead of him going outside through the main hospital doors, despite knowing that he might be playing with fire, Logan found himself lengthening his stride to catch up with her. Or perhaps he needed the challenge to reassure himself that he was still in control?

'Looks like we're heading in the same direction,' he said.

'I know. Weird, huh?'

There might have been the tiniest note of sarcasm in her words but Ella was smiling. Radiating happiness, in fact. She was walking perfectly normally beside him but Logan could almost imagine her starting to skip at any moment and…it was rather nice to be close to someone who was this happy.

'You look like you've had a good day.'

'The best.' Ella nodded.

'You did well with that nuchal arm delivery on the twins.' Logan cleared his throat. 'I hope you didn't think I was interfering by poking my head in.'

'Not at all.' Ella's smile was understanding this time. 'I would have done the same thing. Multiple births are a lot more common these days but they're still magical, aren't they?'

The signal to cross the busy road began flashing red as they got to the traffic lights so they stopped, side by side. Logan was shaking his head.

'They're risky,' he said. 'The chance of complications for both the birth and the babies are also multiplied. Stuff of nightmares for both the doctors and the parents.' He pressed the button again, as if it might make the traffic lights change more quickly. 'And that's only the start. I can't imagine how hard it must be once they leave hospital.'

'It's magical,' Ella said firmly. 'I love everything about them.'

'Maybe you'll be lucky enough to have some yourself.'

'No, thanks.' Ella set off as soon as the lights changed. 'Been there, done that.'

'*What?*'

'Oh, not me, personally.' She threw a grin over her shoulder. 'It was my mother who had the babies. The fertility treatment she had worked a bit too well and she had non-identical triplet boys. Mick, Jimmy and Eddie. I was eight when they turned up.'

'Wow...'

'I adored them,' Ella said. 'Mum needed all the help she could get and I was kind of like another mother. When they started crawling, they'd follow me round like a row of little ducks.'

An eight-year-old who was being a second mother? Logan had to wonder how much Ella had missed out on a normal childhood after her siblings had arrived en masse. Her adolescence must have been rather different to her peers as well. Had she been babysitting while her friends were all out having a good time?

'Where are they now?'

'All over the place. Mick and Jimmy are both junior doctors, currently being overworked in London and Newcastle but they're planning to move on soon. Eddie's a paramedic and working in Australia.'

'Sounds like they all got inspired into a medical career by their big sister.' Logan followed Ella as she unlocked the front door of the doctors' residence and went inside.

'I think it's more about what we all went through when Mum got sick. I was at university, doing my nursing training, so I wasn't around enough, but they were all still at home and it hit hard.'

'They don't sound like they're keen on settling down anywhere any time soon either.'

'They lost their dad not long after Mum

died so it kind of felt like the family's roots got pulled out and there were only sad memories left. I'm not surprised they've all drifted away, looking for a new place to make a fresh start.'

'Wait a minute...' Logan was frowning. '*Their* dad?'

'He was my stepdad.' Ella paused at the bottom of the staircase. 'Mum and I were on our own till I was about five. He was more than happy to adopt me and be my dad but he desperately wanted a kid of his own as well, preferably a boy, so that's why Mum did the fertility treatment.'

'And you set out to be a nurse?'

'Then I decided I wanted to be a doctor.' Ella nodded. 'A paediatrician. But somewhere along the line I realised that you can have too much of a good thing. Obstetrics is perfect. I still adore babies but I prefer the mothers to be *my* patients. And there's no way I want any babies of my own. As I said, been there, done that. With bells on.'

She was heading upstairs now. 'I'm lucky,' she added. 'Most people don't get to appreciate real freedom until they're middle-aged.'

Freedom? So he'd been right in thinking that Ella's childhood had been overwhelmed by responsibilities? Was that why she had a penchant for things that were a little childish now? And why she still got so much joy from being around babies and thought that the arrival of more than one at a time was magical?

Ella Grisham had a big heart, Logan decided, but there was an undercurrent to her story that struck him as being sad. She considered herself to be free now but...wasn't she also lonely? She was capable of meaningful emotional connection to others but if she kept flitting from place to place and never settling it was unlikely that she was going to find it. And maybe that was exactly why she was living her life as she was. It was really none of his business.

He didn't want to get involved and it was possible he'd heard too much of her life story already.

He felt in his pocket for his key as they walked towards the big arched window at the end of the hallway on the second floor. And then he felt his other pocket.

'Oh...no...'

'What's wrong?' Ella had her key in her hand and was about to unlock her own door.

'I have a horrible feeling I left my keys on the kitchen bench this morning. I remember thinking I'd better not forget them because it's too easy to just go out and shut the door and lock it automatically with that snib lock. But I was in a bit of a rush and then my phone rang...'

'Dougal can let you in. Oh...' Ella bit her lip. 'It was this time last week that he was out taking his mother grocery shopping, wasn't it?'

'I can't call him and make him rush back.' Logan sighed. 'It's not the first time this has happened. I have suggested they change the fitting so you have to use a key to lock them as well as open them.' He turned to pick up an envelope that had been on the hall table beside his door.

'That's a fat letter.'

'It'll be photos. I wanted prints of ones I took of my barn the other day. I'm planning to choose the best ones for marketing purposes.'

Ella had unlocked her door. 'Why don't you come in and show me while you wait for Dougal to get back? Returning the favour of not being left in the hallway is the least I can do.' She pushed her door open but stood back—an invitation for Logan to go in first.

He shrugged and accepted the invitation. And then he smiled. 'If you're hitting on me,

Dr Grisham,' he said dryly, 'I need to warn
you that it's doomed to failure. I'm already
married—to my work—and I'm not about to
get distracted.'

It was the first time he'd heard Ella laugh
and the sound followed him as he walked into
her apartment, as joyous as the sight of her
dancing had been. There was something beneath the pleasure of that sound, however.
This was a private joke, wasn't it?

A link that nobody else would understand
that had the effect of creating a connection
on a personal level that had come from no-
where. It had nothing to do with any attraction he'd been aware of with Ella but, despite
Logan having dealt with and buried that un-
wanted reaction to his locum, the two things
were mingling and somehow that alchemy
was making them both bigger. Brighter...

There was nothing very personal about the
apartment Ella had been inhabiting for a week
now, apart from her laptop and a couple of
books and a small framed photograph that
she'd put on top of the almost empty book-
shelf.

Logan paused as he went past the shelf.
'I'm guessing these are your brothers?'

'The babies.' Ella grinned as she nodded. 'None of them was over four pounds when they were born but they've kind of grown up now, haven't they? That was the last time we were all in the same place,' she added. 'Nearly three years ago now.'

She blew out a breath as a beat of missing her family came from left field. But staying in one place long enough to allow for a family reunion to be organised was getting more and more difficult with all of them chasing their own careers and personal freedom. And that was exactly what Ella loved so much about her life, wasn't it—that freedom?

'I think I'm still recovering from the over-powering dose of testosterone, to be honest,' she added lightly. 'It's much more manage-able getting together with a group video call. Have a seat. I can make some coffee. Or tea? I've got some wine, even. I went to the super-market yesterday.' It felt as if Ella was talking too much but she wanted to distract Logan. She'd said too much already about her family, which was probably why she'd found herself suddenly feeling…what…a bit lost?

'You choose.' Logan sat down at the table by the window that was right beside the small kitchen. He ripped the envelope open and was spreading photographs on the table by the time Ella had pulled the cork from the bottle of red wine and found two glasses in a cupboard.

'They're not real wine glasses, sorry. I'm guessing they didn't think it was appropriate to encourage visiting doctors to drink anything stronger than water but, hey… I'm celebrating. Here's to my first multiple birth in Aberdeen.'

Logan picked up the glass tumbler and touched it to the side of Ella's. 'May they all be as joyous as the first,' he said. 'And that you always have a corridor to dance in.'

His tone was so dry that it took a moment for Ella to process the odd toast and, when she did, she almost choked on her sip of wine. He'd seen her doing that happy dance on the way to the locker room? Just how often was she going to embarrass herself in front of this man who always seemed so in control? And serious.

Except…he'd made a joke, hadn't he? About her hitting on him. Twisting that warning she'd thrown at him when they'd first met, and it had been funny. A joke that nobody else would understand. She liked that. It gave them the kind of link that could be the spark of a genuine friendship.

She could only be grateful that Logan had no idea of how attracted she'd been to him that first evening. Ella was also grateful that the fact that he'd changed his mind about letting her work with him as part of the emergency response team had given them a professional connection that made it inappropriate to allow that attraction to be rekindled.

It had definitely helped that they'd both been so busy that their paths hadn't crossed away from work. Until this evening. When Logan had seen her dancing. When he'd walked home with her and she'd shared far too much personal information about her background. At least he'd also seen her coping with what could have been a problem in that twin birth. What was needed now was to steer him away from anything more about her. It was Logan's turn to share.

'So...' Ella put her glass to one side and shifted some photographs to her side of the small table. 'This is the barn that was fabulous enough to make you pretty much live and work in the same place?'

'I had to sell the place I was in to buy the

barn and to fund at least enough of a conversion to make it habitable.'

'Where is it? An easy commute to the city?'

'Thanks to Queen's being on the west side of the city, it's no more than twenty-five minutes if the traffic lights are in a good mood.'

'You'd spend a lot longer than that getting from one suburb to another in London.' Ella was arranging photos in front of her. She opened her mouth to say something about the property but found herself lost for words for a long moment.

The barn was stunning—a huge L-shaped stone and slate building that looked as if it had been there for hundreds of years. There was a crescent of forest behind it and a meadow in front that dipped over a bank to a picturesque pond with fronds of weeping willow reflected in perfectly still water.

'Oh...' Ella found a close-up picture of the pond and her awed silence was broken. 'There's a *duck*. A *Jemima Puddle-Duck* sort of duck.' She sighed happily. 'My favourite.' She glanced up to find Logan smiling at her.

'I had a feeling you'd like that.'

It wasn't that lopsided, half-reluctant smile

she'd seen on Logan's face before. This was almost a grin.

'It's gorgeous,' Ella admitted. 'And you're not going to have any trouble selling it. Especially if that duck is still there as the finishing touch.' She gave Logan a curious glance. 'Are you sure you don't want to turn it into your for ever home?'

Logan sidestepped the glance. 'Maybe I've discovered I'm not a "for ever home" sort of person. Kind of like not being a "settling down" kind of person except for the most important aspect of life.'

'Which is?' Ella was reaching for more photographs.

'A career,' Logan responded, as if the answer was obvious. 'Something that gives you a reason to get up in the morning and a reason to feel like you've done your best to make the world a slightly better place by the time you go to bed at night.'

Ella didn't dare try to catch his gaze as he finished speaking. She could feel an almost overwhelming shadow of something sad hanging over those words but she didn't want to try and analyse it because she knew it might make her question her own lifestyle choices and she didn't want to do that. She was happy.

Happy enough to have been dancing a very short time ago.

She picked up a photo. 'The interior of this barn is amazing.'

'Are you kidding? It hasn't got a floor. The windows are just holes in the stonework and part of the roof has collapsed. There's actually a skeleton of a cow in one corner behind an internal division and a massive pile of musty straw and manure. I suspect the whole mess probably dates back to the eighteenth century.'

Ella waved a hand dismissively. 'You've got to use your imagination. You'd have to work around any limitations that will be in place given that it must have an historical listing, but I'm sure you could leave the stonework of that whole end as it is and build in an open fireplace. You could have stone floors or reclaimed Victorian pine maybe. I'd make a huge living, dining, kitchen area along the whole length from that end and put in a mezzanine floor at the other end that would lead to upstairs bedrooms in the L part of the footprint that would be right under those gorgeous beams.'

Ella was rearranging the photos in front of her, loving the ideas that were crowding her brain and different enough to anything she'd been thinking about all day to be complete recreation. 'It's a good thing that the roof needs repair because you could put in skylights. Solar panels, even. And this…' She tapped an image of a round stone structure with a pointed roof like a witch's hat not far from one end of the barn. 'What is it? A pixie's house?'

'The estate agent thought it might have been a grain silo.'

'You could make that a feature of an outdoor courtyard, with tables and a barbecue for entertaining. Open it up enough to make it like a summer house, with squashy old couches inside, or an antique day bed, so that you could just lie there and watch the ducks on the pond.' Ella laughed aloud. 'I'd find an old weathervane in the shape of a duck and put it on the tippy top of the roof.'

Aware of a sudden silence when she finally stopped talking, Ella looked up to find Logan staring at her.

'I *can* almost see it,' he said slowly. 'I think I saw maybe two percent of what you've described when I saw the property in the first place, but I could never have put it into words like you just have. And none of the architects I've spoken to in the last two years has ever made it sound like it would be worth the effort—and cost—of doing all the work.'

Ella couldn't look away from his eyes, even though she knew she shouldn't be holding eye contact like this. But while she'd noticed how intense a gaze they could deliver, she'd never really noticed their colour—a soft brown with notes of gold that made her think of autumn leaves or walnut shells. It was more than their colour that had captured her, however. It was an emotional note that looked like…hope? No…more like yearning. Something she'd said had touched a chord. It made her wonder if there was something that Logan Walsh wanted very much but he didn't know how to find it.

She dragged her gaze away, swallowing what felt like a lump in her throat. 'You never know,' she said as lightly as she could manage. 'You might change your mind about keeping the barn.'

But Logan shook his head. 'If I haven't found the time or motivation in the last two years, I'm not going to let it hang around my neck like a millstone.'

'What made you buy it in the first place?' Ella was genuinely curious. 'How did you find it?'

Logan shrugged. 'I was driving home from taking a seminar in Fort William and I'd always wanted to drive the Old Military Road through the Cairngorms National Park and it seemed the perfect time. I stopped for a break at one point and I saw a *For Sale* sign with an arrow pointing up a lane so I thought I'd stretch my legs and see what was hiding behind the hedges. There was no one there. It was just me and the barn. In an overgrown meadow with a pond that had ducks on it and...'

Ella wanted to hug herself. 'You fell in love with it,' she said softly.

Logan shook his head, giving Ella a glance that told her exactly how ridiculous that suggestion was. It was reminiscent of the glare he'd treated her to more than once now but Ella wasn't bothered. Maybe it was unconscious—an unfortunate expression of being thoughtful in a professional environment. And quite possibly a warning not to get too close in a personal sense? Simply a defence mechanism?

What was he protecting? Ella wondered. And why?

'It was a pleasant spot, that's all,' Logan said. 'It seemed like a good investment.' He reached for his wine glass and took a long swallow. 'I should get you to help me with writing an advertisement for the place, though. You could inspire anyone to take on the conversion.'

'I could probably come up with more ideas if I actually walked around the place. I could do a few sketches, even.'

'Really? You'd do that?'

'It's a hobby.' Ella shrugged. 'Maybe it's because I was desperate for a doll's house when I was a kid. It was always on the top of my list for Father Christmas but it never happened. I wouldn't have had time to play with it once the babies arrived, of course, and they would have destroyed it by the time they started moving. I'd draw pictures, though, when I needed some quiet time and then I discovered house hunting and renovation programmes on TV and that was when I fell in love with barns.'

Logan finished his wine. 'I'll take you out to see it as soon as we've both got a day off. Keep the photos in the meantime.' He was smiling as he got to his feet. 'I feel like I'm about to get a major weight lifted from my shoulders. When I've sold it, I can go looking for a property in the city. An apartment or house that I can move straight into that will feel like a real home.' Logan checked his watch. 'I expect Dougal will be back by now. I should be able to get back into my apartment now.'

Ella watched him turn away. Yeah...maybe that was what Logan was yearning for.

A 'real' home.

Maybe he needed to settle somewhere to feel grounded.

Ella needed to not have any ties in order to feel free.

They were so different. So why did it feel as if they had a connection that went a lot deeper than a passion for the same work?

It was something else Ella didn't want to try and analyse. And reminding herself of their shared work was the perfect escape route.

'There was something I've been wanting to ask you about,' she said.

'Shoot...' Logan was heading for the door. 'I'll owe you a huge favour if you can help me offload the barn.'

'It's about that course you teach on obstetric emergencies. The one-day seminar you take to ambulance stations and rural hospitals?'

'What about it?'

'Well… I've done locums in places where there's a huge lack of specialist backup for midwives and paramedics. I've done my best to do some training but I'd love to put something more structured together one day. Have you got an instruction manual I could have a look at?'

'Not exactly.' Logan made a face. 'That's something else on my to-do list. I've got notes. And lists. And some handouts for course attendees, but a lot of it's just in my head. I'll tell you about it when we've got a bit of time. Maybe when I take you out for that tour of the barn?'

'I'll look forward to it,' Ella said.

She meant it too. A period of time to talk about and to indulge in the two things she loved the most—her job and her favourite hobby. Put them together with the company of a very attractive man and there was nothing about the prospect not to love.

Ella didn't do one of those silly little dances

when the door had closed behind Logan but that didn't mean she wasn't happy.

She was happier than she could remember being in a very long time, in fact. Excited even, and it didn't really matter which element of the expedition Logan had promised was responsible for this level of anticipation, whether it was an in-depth discussion of managing obstetric emergencies, playing with ideas for a barn conversion or enjoying the company of possibly the most attractive man Ella had ever met. Surely there was nothing wrong in simply enjoying this wonderful fizzy feeling without overthinking it?

CHAPTER FIVE

ELLA WASN'T AT all disappointed by the car Logan was driving when he pulled up in front of the doctors' residence where she was waiting, as arranged, in the early afternoon of her next day off nearly a week later. She had been wondering if he might turn up from where he rented a garage in either a flashy sports car or a luxury late-model sedan but his vehicle was a practical SUV—the kind that could be relied on to do whatever was needed but wouldn't stand out on the motorway. A bit scratched and dented in places but quietly capable. Perfect even, as far as traits that mattered were concerned.

A bit like Logan Walsh himself?

'Right on time,' she said as she opened the passenger door and climbed in. 'I like that.'

She also liked what Logan was wearing, although she certainly wasn't going to tell him that. He had well-worn jeans on and a plain black tee shirt but what took his outfit to a very different level was the ancient-looking leather jacket he had on top. Racer style, with a neck strap instead of a collar and no flashy metal to be seen. Even the zips were hidden. It was the kind of jacket a lot of men might wear to try and look cool but Ella had the impression that Logan would look just as comfortable and confident if he was wearing the most boring anorak on earth.

He waited for Ella to put her bag on the floor and reach for her safety belt. He clearly didn't have the same reticence about commenting on what someone was wearing.

'You've got the llamas on again,' he said.

'These are alpacas,' Ella corrected. 'Classic Peruvian design, probably because it's made out of alpaca wool.'

'What's the difference?' Logan was watching for a gap in the traffic to pull out.

'Llamas are much bigger, have a longer face and their ears are kind of banana-shaped. But you're right, there's not much difference from a distance. I don't think I'd like to wear something knitted from llama wool, though. It would be too scratchy.'

Logan's sideways glance was curious. 'You

seem to know a lot about this. Are camelids another odd hobby of yours?'

Ella grinned at him. 'By "odd", I take it you mean "interesting"?'

He was smiling but busy watching the road ahead of them. 'Absolutely. And I'm very lucky you don't have normal hobbies. I'm looking forward to seeing what you think of the barn.'

'I'm not that into alpacas,' Ella confessed. 'They're not in the same league as dogs or ducks when it comes to rescuing them, but I did have a great time hiking the Incan trail to Machu Picchu a few years ago. This jumper was a souvenir and, I have to say, it's proving useful already in this Scottish climate.' She looked at a signpost they were passing. 'We're heading for Balmoral?'

'Well, we're going in that direction and following the River Dee but it's less than halfway to Balmoral. The closest town is Banchory so it's no more than thirty minutes away even if there's traffic in the city. Ideal for someone that doesn't mind a bit of a commute.'

'It's good.' Ella nodded happily. 'It gives you enough time to start telling me about the course. What's the scope of things that you cover?'

'Depends who I'm talking to,' Logan said. 'It's an intensive one-day seminar so it needs to deliver the information and practical training that is most likely to be of benefit and save lives. So, for example, if I'm talking to paramedics we might put more emphasis on emergencies that can evolve very rapidly, like a placental abruption following trauma or a cord prolapse at the start of labour. Unexpected out-of-hospital deliveries can mean that paramedics might need to manage a severe post-partum haemorrhage or neonatal life support too.'

'And something like complications from a breech delivery or shoulder dystocia are more likely to happen well into labour, which has given the mother more time to get to a hospital,' Ella observed. 'So that would be something that midwives or ED docs might want to brush up on.'

'Exactly. I've got great manikinsto practice the manoeuvres for correcting a shoulder dystocia.'

'I've got an excellent video tutorial that helped me when I was learning to deal with a nuchal arm breech birth complication scenario like the second twin the other day. I could send you a link?' Ella was enjoying the more rural views now they'd left the city behind them.

'That would be great. And I need to send you the draft of a paper I'm working on, because you'll be a co-author.'

'Oh...?' Ella turned a startled glance to Logan but he was focused on the road ahead so she allowed her gaze to rest on his profile a moment or two longer, taking in the strong angles of his face and lines that suggested he frowned more often than he smiled. The sombre tone didn't detract from his attractiveness, however. Quite the opposite...

'One of a few because I'm including everyone that made a significant contribution to the case, but it'll be directed to an obstetric publication so you'll be the first co-author.'

Ella blinked. That was quite an honour, considering Logan Walsh's prominence in the field and that she was only a locum colleague. 'Is it a case presentation?' she guessed. 'For the resuscitative hysterotomy?'

'Yeah... Success stories can be important. They may well contribute to someone making a decision to do a procedure that is, let's face it, more than a little daunting but making the decision in time might make the difference between life and death.'

'Mmm…' The sound Ella made was thoughtful. She turned to look at the countryside rolling past but, in reality, she was completely focused on the man sitting so close to her.

If Logan had been daunted when faced with that decision on performing such an invasive procedure when the odds were against it being successful, he hadn't shown it and that confidence and control of the situation had been pivotal to the entire team that day. How good was he at hiding his feelings? Ella wondered—a thought that was instantly followed by wondering why he was alone in life and whether anybody had ever got close enough to be allowed to know what was going on in his head. Or his heart?

He was several years older than Ella, which would make him close to being forty years old. Had he been married before—to something other than his work? It was unthinkable to ask such personal questions of this … what was the word that summed Logan up? Taciturn? Yeah…that was it. A good Scottish characteristic. Ella stole another glance in his direction, imagining Logan wearing a kilt, with all the traditional accessories like a sporran and socks and a hat and a fly plaid over his shoulder with maybe a brooch to pin it. Would he be traditional enough not to wear anything underneath his kilt?

And...there it was again. That spear of deliciousness deep in her belly that was undeniably sheer physical desire.

Stop it, Ella chided herself. *You're too close. He might notice and how embarrassing would that be?*

She needed to tap into the professional space that was more than acceptable to share but she couldn't think of anything to say. Thank goodness Logan could.

'I think the paper will create some interest,' he said. 'It's very unusual for both a mother and baby to survive an RH and in my discussion I've talked about how part of the success in a case like this can be due to the pre-hospital management by paramedics and that up-to-date training is vital to maintain.'

Ella was thoroughly back in a professional zone now. 'You don't mean having paramedics *doing* an RH, do you?'

'Why not? If a specialist paramedic in critical care can do a thoracotomy for a tension pneumothorax and associated cardiac arrest, why not an RH?' But then Logan shook his head a little. 'That wasn't what I meant, though.'

'What did you mean?'

'I suspect the course that the paramedics who brought Iona in had just done may have made a difference in this particular case. They knew to use a higher hand position on the sternum and to manually displace the uterus to take pressure off the IVD and aorta. A different crew in a different place might have still been using the old recommendation to have the mother in a thirty-degree, left lateral position that makes effective chest compressions almost impossible.'

This was good. Ella wasn't thinking of anything personal to do with Logan now. She was so back in that resuscitation room in the emergency department she could actually feel an echo of the calm control that had emanated from Logan.

'And you knew how fast you needed to make the decision to do the procedure,' she said quietly. 'You had the baby out in less than five minutes.'

'We did.'

Ella could allow herself a small glow of pride in his change of pronoun, even though it could be considered a grey area between professional and personal interaction. Like heading off to see Logan's personal possession of a barn, even though what they were talking about was purely professional?

'But those recommended time frames are also outdated,' Logan added. 'There are reports of babies being delivered alive up to thirty minutes after CPR's been started and mothers have survived up to fifteen minutes.'

'It's still got to be a good thing to do it as early as possible.' Ella bit her lip. 'I know Iona's doing well but it's still going to be a long road to a complete recovery, isn't it?'

Logan nodded. 'I spent some time with her on my ward round this morning. She's probably going to be kept in as long as her baby's in NICU, for some intensive therapy and rehabilitation.'

He knew the baby's name was Finlay. Was he avoiding using it because he was deliberately creating distance? It couldn't be because he didn't like babies—he was an obstetrician, for heaven's sake.

'I was a bit shocked by her level of disability when she was first awake,' Ella confessed. 'She was having a lot of difficulty speaking and she was quite agitated. I could see how hard it was for her family.'

'She's making good progress. She's lost a lot of her vocabulary and has trouble naming things, but her husband tells me that as soon as he's told her the word it's back in her memory. She's frustrated and is fighting a fatigue that makes it hard to stay awake, but she's less emotionally labile and apparently determined to recover from the left-sided weakness. She wants to be able to hold her baby.'

He was doing it again. Creating distance by not using names and talking about people as if he was dictating clinical notes. It made Ella feel a little rebellious.

'I try and find time every day to go and visit Finlay,' she said. 'He's the most adorable baby ever. He's off CPAP now, although he's being carefully monitored for any apnoeic episodes, and he's starting to learn to suck from a bottle. Did you know that Iona's being helped to express breastmilk for him? The plan is to let her try breastfeeding soon. I'm so excited about that. I bet she and Gregor are too.'

Logan didn't appear to be listening. He had turned off the road and they were bumping down a rough narrow lane between hedgerows. She could hear the warning sounds of startled birds but wasn't going to take that as a warning to drop the subject.

'Have you been to see him?'

'No. I've been getting regular updates on his condition, of course. The data will be included in a table in the paper I'm writing on the RH.'

Maybe Logan could sense Ella's disapproval of his lack of excitement over Finlay's progress. He broke the silence as he slowed the car when they reached the end of the lane and had turned to see the barn and meadow and pond—as if one of those photographs, or maybe a landscape painting, had just come to life.

'NICU is not one of my favourite places,' he said quietly.

The undercurrent to his words suggested that Logan had seen too many newborn babies that hadn't survived—maybe from cases that haunted him—but still Ella said nothing. She could feel a compelling peacefulness of the scene in front of them inviting them in. She could also feel quite certain that Logan had just told her something that was intensely personal and private and, as much as she wanted to know more, this felt like a test. Could she be trusted not to pry into places he wasn't ready to show her, no matter how curious she might be?

Yes. She could.

And maybe Logan already knew that. He'd already invited her into a personal space, hadn't he? Ella had the feeling that she might be the first person he had confessed his preference to avoid the NICU. She was also possibly the first person, other than an architect perhaps, to set foot in this little patch of countryside since Logan had fallen in love with it enough to buy it.

Oops... Since he'd discovered an out of the way, 'pleasant spot' and convinced himself it might be a good financial investment.

She opened her door, hiding her smile. 'We'd better make the most of the sunshine,' she said. 'I'm not sure I like the look of those clouds rolling in.'

Logan hadn't been out here for months. Good grief...was it coming up to almost a year since his last visit?

He'd never been here with anyone else either, come to think of it. He'd been alone when he'd discovered it and he'd dealt with the estate agent and the purchase without feeling the need to see it again. He'd sent architects the directions to get there and told them where the key to the barn was hidden but he'd never managed to be available to be there at the same time.

Had he wanted to keep this place a purely personal retreat? Or had he, perhaps, been unconsciously worried that the spell it seemed to cast on him whenever he was here would be somehow tainted by sharing it with someone else?

If he had, he'd been very wrong.

Sharing it with Ella was...well, it was a bit of a revelation, to be honest.

He suspected that Ella had no idea just how much her changing expressions—and her eyes—revealed about how she was feeling. And if anyone was capable of something as ridiculous as falling head over heels in love with a property he might have known it would be Ella.

She was enchanted from the moment he reached into the hollow trunk of an ancient oak tree to find the old iron key that had probably been hand forged by the same blacksmith who'd created the heavy lock on the rustic wooden door. She caught her bottom lip between her teeth as he pushed that door open, as if she was holding her breath, and then she actually wrapped her arms around her body when she was standing inside the cavernous space with misty rays of sunshine pouring in through the small, high windows.

Those dark eyes of hers that were such a good match for her hair colour were shining just as brightly. Logan had become used to only seeing her hair tied back at work so it was a bit disconcerting to see it hanging in the long, loose waves that had caused that totally inappropriate thought about her riding a horse with nothing but her hair to cover her body. It was even more disconcerting to see the astonishing array of emotions in her reaction to this historic building.

'Those beams and the trusses...they're incredible. Hand-hewn. Maybe oak, or elm or chestnut wood? Oh...can you imagine that mezzanine floor with the bedrooms having those beams on their ceilings? Close enough to see the marks that someone made with an axe or an adze? To be able to *touch* them?'

Logan was being sucked in again, like he had been the other night when Ella was full of ideas about a conversion project—until she'd accused him of falling in love with the property, which let him escape straight back to a safe distance. It felt more dangerous, some-how, hearing the passion in her voice while they were physically inside this building.

He needed to remember that he'd learned long ago not to play mental games with per-sonal 'what ifs' or 'if onlys'. That it was so much safer to think about facts rather than fantasies. To push forward and focus on doing what mattered to the best of his ability.

His work.

The error of purchasing a project that would require too much of his time and money had taught Logan a good lesson. He hadn't realised the effect it would have to be forced into a space where you had to dream about the future and he'd quickly found that doing so could unlock doors he'd rather not go through, thanks very much. He needed a place to live that would help him do his work and live his life by *not* being a distraction or possibly even an ordeal.

'I still think it should be at the short end of the L shape,' Ella said. 'But I didn't see that stone partition in the photos. There's room for a stone staircase to lead up to the mezzanine level and that might be the perfect place to build in a gorgeous big open fireplace.'

Okay…he couldn't stop himself seeing that.

Not when the solid stonework was right in front of him. He could actually imagine the roaring flames and a couple of super comfortable leather sofas in front of it. And Ella was sitting there, with a glass of wine in her hand. Smiling…

'I'm going to take some more photos.' Ella pulled her phone out of her shoulder bag. 'I've got a sketch pad too, but you probably don't want to hang around long enough for me to do any drawing here.'

'Do whatever you need,' Logan said.

'What would *you* need,' Ella asked, 'if you were going to be living here?'

'But I'm not going to be living here.'

Ella gave him a strange look. 'Help me out here, Logan. Play the game. It'll make it so much easier to make this real. Otherwise, you'll only get my ideas and I can probably make it appeal to a much wider market if I know what you'd want.'

Logan shrugged. If it was going to help get rid of this place, being temporarily uncomfortable would be a reasonable price to pay.

'What's important to you?' Ella asked. 'Outside of work, I mean.'

Logan was silent for a moment, genuinely at a loss to think of something that wasn't connected to his career that was important enough to need catering for in a dwelling.

'Do you love books?' Ella prompted. 'Would a library with a lovely old desk be attractive? It could be tucked behind the stone partition and the fire.'

Logan could see that too. Shelves and shelves of books, with a whole section for the old medical textbooks he loved to collect that were sitting in boxes in storage. Maybe there were floorboards of the dark grainy wood of reclaimed pine Ella had mentioned, with an old Persian-style carpet square in a lovely deep shade of red.

Ella's voice broke into that glimmer of an indoor retreat Logan had never imagined having.

'Are you a secret gourmet cook? How 'bout a kitchen with an Aga and a butler's sink and a pantry built into the corner so it's got stone walls, which will make it a cool store as well. Or…even better—that space could be the wine cellar?'

No. A pantry would be better. Stocked with food that would simmer slowly in the Aga to make something delicious. He pulled in a deep breath through his nose, as if he could actually smell it cooking.

Ella didn't seem to mind that he wasn't saying anything aloud. She was turning in a circle, looking up at the too-small windows. 'What do you want to see as a view? The forest? Or, if we were allowed, we could put in huge windows or French doors and that way we could see the little pixie house and the pond from almost any corner of the house. I think...' Ella was frowning now. 'I've lost my sense of direction. Can we go outside and have a look?'

'Good idea...' Logan's head was starting to spin. It was getting far too easy to summon the images that Ella's words were creating and they came with a sting in their tail of doubts that were creeping in. Maybe he *did* want to live here after all. Maybe he'd forgotten what it was that had captured him that day he'd wandered in the direction of the 'For Sale' sign.

But, as perfect as Ella made it sound, would he want to be here? Alone? Was it the way she kept saying 'we'?

If we were allowed...

We could see the little pixie house...

Maybe it was being in Ella's company that was not only casting the spell again but bringing it to life in a way that was...disturbing, that was what it was. Logan was aware of an emotional response that was strong enough to be making it difficult to keep reined in with his usual ease. It would be easier outside, he decided. Especially with the chill of the breeze that had sprung up and the way dark clouds were swiftly moving to mask the sunshine.

They had to push through knee-high grass and weeds between the long wall of the barn and the pond. They walked past the small circular building to get closer to the pond and then both turned back. Logan could feel the first drops of rain starting to fall but Ella didn't seem to notice. She was taking photographs and then simply staring and Logan could almost see the ideas of that outdoor courtyard featuring the pixie house forming in her head.

He almost groaned aloud as he caught himself automatically referring to it as the 'pixie house' and he needed to shift his gaze so Ella didn't catch him watching the changing expressions on her face with such fascination. Turning his head, he gave a huff of laughter.

'There you go…' he said. 'Your duck's come to say hello. With a friend.'

'Oh…' Ella's face lit up. 'I wish I'd thought

to bring some crusts of bread. I'll have to re-member next time…'

Next time…?

Something like pleasure at the thought of being here again with Ella added itself to the strange mix of slightly out-of-control emotions Logan was grappling with but the distraction of the sudden, unexpected downpour of rain as the heavens opened was enough to kill the moment.

'Oh, my God…' Ella shoved her phone into her bag and wrapped her arms around it protectively as she turned to look towards the closest form of shelter, which was the pixie house. 'Has it got a doorway?'

It did. A narrow, low door space that they could just squeeze through, but there was plenty of room to stand up once they were inside. They could hear the heavy raindrops pelting the slates above their heads and they stood close together so they could both see out of the gap in the stone walls, through the veil of water falling outside to where the ducks were still floating on the now ruffled surface of the pond.

'I'm soaked,' Ella said. 'How did that happen so fast?' She pulled at the front of her jumper and drops of water flicked onto where

Logan had his hand on the edge of the gap, which made him turn away from watching for a break in the downpour. Her hair looked almost as wet as the night Logan had found her unable to get into her apartment and she even had drops of water caught on the tangle of her dark eyelashes.

And there it was…

A blast of the sexual attraction he thought he'd dealt with more than a week ago and it was the straw that broke the camel's back as far as controlling his emotions went. Because Ella was staring back at him and he was quite certain that he was seeing a reflection of that attraction in her eyes.

He wanted to kiss her.

He was almost sure that that was what Ella wanted as well.

But that wanting was so powerful it felt dangerous. It might be the hardest thing Logan had done in a very long time but he managed to break that eye contact. He looked outside. There was no sign of the rain letting up but Logan knew what would happen if they stayed in this small space, and suddenly he wasn't at all sure that Ella wanted it as much as he did.

'It doesn't look like this rain is going to

stop any time soon,' he said. 'Shall we make a run for it?'

He definitely needed to make a run for it—and not just to get out of the rain.

CHAPTER SIX

HAD SHE IMAGINED IT?

Or, by the power of wishful thinking, had Ella somehow seen how she had been feeling herself reflected in Logan's eyes?

She could have sworn he'd wanted to kiss her as much as she'd wanted him to, but now she was changing her mind.

It had been an awkward trip back from the property. They'd got even wetter by the time they'd locked up, put the key back in its hiding place in the hollow tree and reached the shelter of the car. With the heaters on the windows had steamed up and Logan had to focus on his driving. He also turned the radio on and Ella was treated to an exceedingly dull in-depth discussion about a recent football match and more than one controversial decision the referee had made so she kept her head down and scrolled through the photos she had taken in and outside the barn.

The rain had clearly set in for the rest of the day and, after having a long, hot shower and washing her hair, Ella couldn't see any point in getting properly dressed again, especially when it was already dark enough to need the lights on, so she put on her pyjamas and some fluffy socks even though it was only four p.m. The apartment was nice and warm and, having combed out her hair, she curled up on the couch with her sketchpad and pencils and quickly became lost in the pleasure of something creative that was the time out she loved the most.

The knock on her door just after six p.m. startled her enough to make her drop her pencil.

'Who is it?'

'Logan.'

'Oh…' For a moment Ella was tempted to say it wasn't a good time but it wasn't as though her pyjamas were something awful like flannelette with a kitten print or something. They were just leggings and an oversized tee shirt, and she could probably cover up the fact that she wasn't wearing a bra by just peering around the door to see what he wanted.

And…her heart rate had picked up quite noticeably and there was that knot of sensation that was getting ready to fire those spears of that very pleasant physical response to a man she was very much attracted to. Plus Ella was curious. Firstly as to why he was knocking at her door but also because she still had that question burning in the back of her mind.

Had she imagined that he'd been tempted to kiss her?

This was most likely the best chance she was going to get to find the answer to that question so she found herself walking to the door. She forgot to hide behind it, however, being instantly distracted by what she could smell.

'I thought you might be hungry,' Logan said. 'And… I was feeling bad that you got wet. Again.'

As if Ella needed reminding of when he'd found her, soaked to the skin, unable to get into her new apartment. Or being in his apartment, using his towel to dry her hair. Or, most of all, discovering that she was attracted to him more than she had ever been attracted to anyone when she'd first met them, in fact. But maybe the reminder was why she was feeling it so strongly again right now. Enough to make her skin tingle right down to her toes.

'Do you fancy some Thai takeaway?' Logan's smile was an invitation all by itself.

Ella's toes were curling inside those fluffy socks as she took a deep, appreciative sniff. 'That smells *so* good.'

'Spring rolls, chicken satay, drunken noodles and green curry. I've been to this restaurant before and they make the best drunken noodles I've ever tasted…'

Logan's voice—and smile—were trailing away and his eyebrows were rising. Ella couldn't miss the way he deliberately shifted his gaze after it had drifted down to take in her attire. Or lack of it? Had he guessed she wasn't wearing any underwear at all?

It would be polite to acknowledge that she wasn't dressed for company and suggest that he came back in a few minutes but Ella could actually *feel* that Logan was struggling to keep a lid on his reaction.

That she hadn't been imagining a mutual level of attraction between them this afternoon and, dammit…she didn't want to give him the chance to put his barriers up again, the way he had when he'd made her listen to that boring dissection of a football match on their journey home.

'That's the best offer I've had in a very long time.' Ignoring any flickers of doubt, Ella pulled the door open further. 'Do come in.'

This was a bad idea.

But he could hardly tell Ella that he'd made a mistake and he didn't think quickly enough to say he had other commitments, leave her the food and disappear.

And if he was honest...he didn't want to. He might have successfully taken control of the situation this afternoon by making a run for it but he hadn't been able to stop thinking about it ever since and the pull that had made him think up an excuse to knock on Ella's door had been, quite simply, irresistible.

So he followed her into her apartment. He tried—and failed—to think about the fact that she wasn't wearing a bra and her hair was a loose waterfall down her back and all that was in the way of that Lady Godiva fantasy was the thin fabric of a well-worn tee shirt.

Searching desperately for a distraction, he noticed the scattered pencils over sheets of paper on the coffee table.

'You've been sketching already?'

'Mmm…' Ella reached to take the paper carrier bag from Logan's hands. 'Why don't you have a look while I find some plates? And would you like a glass of wine?'

'Yes…but let me help.' Logan couldn't stop himself. Maybe it was the touch of Ella's fingers against his hand as she tried to take hold of the handles of the bag. He dismissed the escape route he'd just been offered and kept hold of it. 'You get the wine,' he said. 'I'll sort the food.'

He put the bag on the bench of the small kitchenette and took out the foil containers with their cardboard lids while Ella took a bottle of wine from the pantry cupboard. Logan had opened an overhead cupboard to find some plates and Ella reached for the glasses that were beside them.

Their hands touched again and they both pulled back to give the other a chance to get what they needed.

But neither of them moved.

There they were, standing so close that Logan wasn't sure if the warmth he was aware of was coming from the hot food on the bench or from Ella's skin and whether the aroma filling his nostrils was from the spices in his favourite cuisine or from Ella's hair. He could almost taste them.

He *wanted* to taste them.

And then he saw the look in Ella's eyes as she lifted her gaze to meet his and he completely forgot all about food. Or wine. Or the sketches on the table. Nothing existed apart from Ella Grisham and a deep, soul-scorching level of…need, that was what it was. It was too strong to be anywhere near the attraction point of a spectrum that included all shades of desire. And it was strong enough to stifle any warning that this might be a bad idea.

He could feel Ella getting closer, as if she was going onto her tiptoes. Or maybe it was because he was dipping his head. Just a little. Not enough to break that eye contact for a long, long moment. Because he needed to be sure that Ella wanted this as much as he did. If that was even possible…

Logan closed his eyes when they were close enough for Ella's face to have become a blur. Time seemed to be moving incredibly slowly. So slowly that he could take the time to let the tip of his nose touch the side of her nose for a heartbeat. For him to touch his lips to the corner of her mouth and then move, still in such slow motion that his bottom lip could feel the dent in her chin and then capture her bottom lip between his so that the tip of his tongue could touch...and taste... the unbelievable softness of her lip.

And then, without warning, time sped up. Perhaps it was the touch of Ella's tongue against *his* lips. Or the way she lifted her arms, lacing her fingers over the nape of his neck. Maybe it was because it felt as if she was losing her balance as she pressed closer, standing on those tippy toes, which made Logan instinctively reach to hold her steady and, as he did, the palm of one of his hands brushed her breast and beneath that thin fabric he could feel a nipple that was as hard as a tiny pebble.

It was most likely a combination of everything, combined with a rising level of a passion that promised to be as unrestrained and intense and joyful as Logan suspected Ella could be. Whatever the catalyst, something exploded so fast there was no time to make conscious decisions. Logan was being swept along in a tide that he'd never felt the like of. With one movement he bent and put an arm behind Ella's knees and scooped her into his arms. His lips found hers again as he turned, but he didn't need more than a glimpse of any obstacles in their way because he knew the layout of this apartment was the same as his own.

He knew where the bedroom was.

Oh…dear Lord…

Talk about being swept off your feet!

Not that Ella was about to try and slow this down. If anything, she wanted it to go faster so it was almost disappointing to find herself gently deposited on the side of her bed instead of being thrown onto her back on the mattress. But then she opened her eyes and found Logan looking down at her. And then he moved his hand to cup the back of her neck and bent down to start kissing her again and she just melted inside. She found the buttons of his shirt beneath her fingers and started undoing them one by one, without breaking those kisses for anything more than a snatch of air or a head tilt so that their lips—and tongues—could explore even more.

And then her fingers reached the band of his jeans so Ella lifted her arms into the air and Logan knew exactly what to do. He took handfuls of the hem of her tee shirt and pulled it up and over her head. He stripped off his own shirt and Ella unfastened the stud on his jeans. She didn't get the chance to slide his zip down, however, because Logan was lifting her to her feet, his hands sliding under the waistband of her leggings to push them down.

His soft oath was almost a huff of laughter.

'Do you often go around with no knickers on, Ella?'

'These are my PJs. You don't wear knickers to bed, do you?'

'I don't wear anything to bed,' Logan admitted.

A beat of silence and then he was shedding his jeans and Ella was kicking herself free of her leggings. She was still standing in front of him and he held her with one arm around her waist as he leaned in to cover her lips with his own. She could feel his other hand sliding down her back, cupping her buttock and then drifting into the gap between their bodies to touch her even more intimately.

Ella gasped, the astonishing flood of sensation taking her so much by surprise that she found herself sinking in to sit on the edge of the bed again, as if her knees were no longer useful. And then she was falling backwards, onto the bed, and Logan was still kissing her—following the movement of her body as if it was a dance and he needed to stay in contact. He was kneeling over her and it could have been all over far too soon except that they caught each other's gaze and the question was almost written in a bubble in the air between them.

'Bedside cabinet,' Ella said. 'Top drawer.'

Breaking the pace of the almost out-of-control passion to make sure they were both protected was a good thing, she decided. It had slowed things down again and Logan was kissing her with the same almost poignant intensity of that first kiss in the kitchen. Ella could have happily stayed in that space for as long as possible but, like it had during those first kisses, a switch seemed to get flicked and they were falling into a very different space where rational thought was overtaken by sensation.

The taste…

The touch…

The exquisite pleasure that built and built until there was no room left to contain it and it could only escape with all the drama this particular climax had promised. And then they were lying side by side, waiting to catch their breath and have their heart rates return to something like a normal level. Logan's arm was under Ella's neck and they were both looking at the ceiling. Until they weren't. Until, by some kind of telepathic signal, they rolled towards each other and kissed once more. A long, slow, delicious kiss…

'All right?' Logan asked softly.

Ella's smile started slowly but she couldn't help it continuing to grow. She wanted to say that she'd never been better. That she'd never had a first time with anyone that had been that good, but instinct told her not to make this into too much of a big deal or Logan would run and hide again. Like he had this afternoon. He'd even said it out loud, hadn't he?

Shall we make a run for it…?

So Ella held his face with both hands and gave him a gentle, short kiss on his lips. 'I'm still hungry,' she told him. 'I think I'm even hungrier than I was before.'

'That food will be stone cold,' Logan groaned.

Ella rolled away to reach for her tee shirt and leggings. 'Isn't that what they invented microwaves for?'

This was exactly the kind of situation that Logan had carefully avoided for more than a decade now. It wasn't that he didn't have a sex life—of course he did—but it was very carefully orchestrated to be a friendship with benefits that always ran its course when his partners either found that he was being totally honest about there being no chance of a permanent relationship and moved on or he needed to escape politely when they made it obvious they were hoping for more.

Any intimate encounters were somewhere that Logan was able to leave at a time of his choice. He never invited them into his home and he never stayed a whole night. He certainly didn't hang around to share a meal with anyone. He'd never chosen someone who lived close to his home, let alone merely a few steps away across a hallway and…oh, no… had he somehow forgotten that he had to *work* with Ella and, unless he actively avoided it, he might see her every day? Several times a day, even.

Logan expected this to be horribly awkward but it wasn't.

Ella was acting as if it was no big deal. As if they hadn't just shared the best sex he'd ever experienced in his life. Logan was still getting faint aftershocks of sensation deep in his belly—like when he watched her use chopsticks to start eating a mouthful of noodles but simply sucked in the ends that hadn't made it inside her mouth.

'Oh, wow…you were right. These are the best drunken noodles ever.'

'Have you tried the curry?' Logan reached for more rice to put in his bowl. 'I hope it's not too spicy for you. I wasn't sure what level of heat you might like.'

'Oh…?' Ella's eyes were dancing. 'I love a bit of heat…'

She reached over and helped herself to a mouthful of food from his dish—as if they were so comfortable in each other's company it was a given that they could share food without asking permission. 'Good guess,' she murmured. 'Why am I not surprised?'

It was obvious Ella was talking about Logan's ability to provide a level of heat that had nothing whatsoever to do with food but even that didn't make things awkward. Until he was helping clean up after their dinner and Logan could feel a clock beginning to tick. It was the logical time for him to excuse himself and go home. A day—and night—that he was never likely to forget was about to end.

Realising that he didn't *want* to go home was a gut feeling that was nothing like one of those pleasurable aftershocks.

'It's time I went home,' he said aloud, for his own benefit as much as Ella's.

Was he hoping that Ella would invite him to stay a bit longer? For a coffee or another glass of wine? Another session of sensational sex, even? If he was hoping for that he was instantly disappointed because Ella's response was a nod as she checked her watch.

'I've got to make a call to Australia soon,' she said. 'It might go on for a while.'

'Australia?'

'I've agreed to take on a six-month locum there for my next position and I think there are a few questions that need answering on both sides.'

'Australia…' It wasn't a question this time. A beat of dismay was the last thing Logan might have expected to feel. 'That's a world away from Aberdeen.'

'Last time I looked, yeah…' Ella was smiling at him. 'But Eddie makes it sound like it's the best place in the world so it's about time I went to see for myself. And if I'm there for long enough we might manage another family reunion. Somewhere amazing…like the Blue Mountains or Tasmania or one of those gorgeous islands on the Great Barrier Reef.'

Logan was completely caught by that smile.

Or perhaps the sparkle in Ella's eyes and the excitement in her voice.

'You really love being free to go anywhere, don't you?' Was he impressed or envious of Ella's lifestyle? Or perhaps there was a bit of relief surfacing. It didn't matter how he felt about what had just happened between them because it wasn't a threat to either of their lifestyles.

'It's the best feeling in the world,' Ella said.

By tacit consent, they were both moving towards her door. In a few seconds Ella was going to open it and Logan could step back into his own world that had nothing like the kind of magic dust this woman seemed to be able to gather and scatter for others to share.

No wonder Logan had never found himself in a situation like this before.

He'd never met anyone like Ella before and he was quite sure he would never meet anyone like her ever again.

She was one of a kind and she wasn't going to be in his life for more than a few weeks so did it matter that he was breaking his own rules and boundaries? He didn't have to worry about a liaison that might not run its course in an amicable fashion because the end date was already built in. There was no need to be already planning a polite escape so there was also no need to take any notice of those faint alarm bells that were ringing in the back of his mind.

Logan paused when Ella opened her door.

'Thanks for dinner,' she said. 'I really enjoyed it.'

He was close enough to make it very easy to touch her cheek with his fingers.

'Thank *you*,' he said softly. 'It wasn't the food that I enjoyed the most.' He traced the line of Ella's jaw, caught her chin and bent his head to kiss her. Slowly. And thoroughly, because he could sense that she was in no hurry to say goodnight.

She looked slightly dazed when he finally lifted his head.

In that beat of silence Logan wondered who was going to be the first to suggest they did it again. Not him, he decided almost instantly. Ella had already made it clear that the sex had been no big deal. This was casual. It probably didn't matter that much to either of them whether or not it was going to happen again. If it did, great… If it didn't, well, that was fine too.

'You working tomorrow?' Ella's voice was

a little rough. She cleared her throat. 'Maybe I'll see you then?'

'Maybe…' Logan moved through the door. Another step and he was almost halfway across the hallway. 'I am working, yes…'

But it did matter, he realised, when he reached his own door and looked over his shoulder to see that Ella was already closing hers, because how much he wanted it to happen again should really be a warning signal. He heard the click of her door lock and blew out a breath when he closed his own door a moment later. He was pretty sure that Ella would welcome another encounter just as much as he would but there was only one way to be sure.

He'd been the one to initiate things this evening by turning up with that food, so if there *was* going to be a next time it would have to be Ella's turn to hit on him.

CHAPTER SEVEN

WAS HE WAITING for her to make the next move?

Ella had fully expected not to have Logan acknowledge any difference due to their relationship becoming somewhat more than simply colleagues. Certainly not at work, anyway. She'd had the impression from the moment she'd met him that he kept his distance and his private life simply that—private. He'd also made it very clear that he wouldn't tolerate distractions of any kind so Ella would have been astonished if she'd been the recipient of meaningful glances across an operating table or patient's bed, or an obvious increase in time together like sharing a lunch break. A fantasy rendezvous involving a lot of kissing and inappropriate touching, in his office or a secluded corner on the hospital roof, perhaps, was the stuff of television soap operas, not real life.

And that was fine by her. She was just as passionate about her career as Logan was about his and this was, after all, only the second day back at work after their very private time together on their shared day off. Like the way Ella had backed off from asking personal questions to let Logan know he could trust her, she was more than happy to give him time to realise she wasn't going to be a distraction at work either.

She wasn't even thinking about him, in fact, when she got paged for a consult in the emergency department, other than a brief flash of realising that the last time she'd been in this part of the hospital had been when Logan had invited her to join him for that OERT response.

'Her name's Beth,' the registrar told her when she arrived. 'She's thirteen weeks pregnant and she's got severe abdominal pain—right lower quadrant. She's convinced she's miscarrying although we've found a healthy heartbeat on ultrasound and there's no blood loss. No fever, she's tachycardic at one forty bpm, has a respiration rate of twenty-four, but she's extremely upset. She lost her first baby at fourteen weeks.'

'Oh, no...' Ella's heart immediately went

out to the patient she was about to see. 'She must be terrified.'

She was. Beth was sobbing when Ella entered the assessment. An older woman sat on a chair beside the bed, her face creased with anxiety.

'Hi, Beth... My name's Ella. I'm one of the obstetric consultants here at Queen's.' Ella grabbed a handful of tissues from a box on the bench and gave them to Beth. 'I know how scary this is,' she said softly. 'But we're going to take very good care of you, okay?'

Beth blew her nose. 'This is my fault. I shouldn't have come up to see Mum. But my GP said I was fine.'

'When did you see your GP?'

'A few days ago for the pain. He said it was probably just wind but he sent me to hospital for an ultrasound because I'd been spotting a bit before that and he knew...he knew...'

'He knew how worried she was,' Beth's mother put in. 'It's only a year ago that Beth lost her first baby. That's why I suggested she came to visit me for a few days while her husband's away for work—so that she wasn't by herself.'

Beth was sobbing again but her cry turned

into an agonised groan. Ella turned to the registrar. 'What has Beth had for the pain?'

'Morphine. Five milligrams.'

'Let's top that up and get on top of this pain.' Ella could see the Luer plug taped to Beth's arm. 'Have you got any blood results back yet?'

'We should have got the full blood count back by now.' The registrar frowned. 'I'll go and check.'

'Thanks.' A high white count might be indicative of an infection and appendicitis was a common cause of lower right quadrant pain but a white count could be elevated in pregnant women anyway and there were many other potential causes, both associated with pregnancy and coincidental. An acute abdomen in a pregnant woman was a challenge and overlapped specialties so Ella was already aware that a consult with a general surgeon could be needed. She asked the nurse to take another set of vital signs as she gave Beth a minute or two for the pain to settle before examining her.

She found Beth's abdomen to be rigid and still very tender despite the morphine and she was saying she felt sick, despite the antinausea medication that had been administered along with the opioid. The pain seemed to be spreading to the upper right quadrant as well, which only added to the differential diagnoses Ella needed to consider. Beth might have kidney stones or an infection, an ovarian cyst might have ruptured and the risk of an ovarian torsion in early pregnancy was already much greater than normal. It could be gallstones or pancreatitis and she wanted to see the blood test results on liver function. She also wanted to do her own ultrasound examination and she was in the process of doing that when both the ED registrar and another consultant came into the room.

The other consultant was Logan. He came up behind Ella to peer at what she was seeing on the screen of the portable ultrasound machine.

'I've got a meeting with ED management,' he said quietly. 'But I heard you were here and I got briefed on the history.'

Ella could feel a sudden tension in her body. It had nothing to do with the unexpected sound of Logan's voice, or the fact that he was standing close enough for her to be aware of the warmth of *his* body. It wasn't associated with any memory of the way Logan had taken over the management of a case she was assessing either—the way he had on the first day they'd met.

'See that?'

'Mmm…' It was a soft sound of agreement that disguised any underlying concern.

There was free fluid in Beth's abdomen. Not a huge amount but enough to be a real concern. Ella angled the transducer to try and get a clearer image.

'Appendicitis?' Logan suggested. His mouth was close enough to her ear for only Ella to hear what he was saying. 'Acute cholecystitis? Ovarian cyst rupture?'

'Can't rule any of them out yet,' she responded. She didn't say it aloud but she knew they were both thinking that urgent surgery might be necessary to both make the diagnosis and treat it. Changing the angle again, she picked up the baby's heartbeat and Logan smiled at the reassuring sound of a baby who wasn't in immediate distress.

'Can you hear that, Beth? That's your baby's heart.'

'I feel sick,' Beth moaned. 'And dizzy…'

'Blood pressure's ninety-five on sixty,' the nurse reported. 'Down from one-ten on seventy. That last recording was only five minutes ago.'

Ella looked up to catch Logan's gaze and she knew that his gut instinct was the same as her own. There was something potentially serious going on here. This abdominal pain might not be associated with the pregnancy but it still had the risk of affecting it and the sooner they could diagnose the problem the better. The best way to rule out the most serious possibilities was by an exploratory laparoscopic investigation.

'I think we're going to need to take a look at what's going on in your tummy,' she told Beth. 'We'll get a general surgeon to come and see you as well, because it might be something that has nothing to do with you being pregnant. The most likely cause is acute appendicitis.'

Beth was crying again. Her mother had gone almost as pale as her daughter. 'An operation? Isn't that dangerous for the baby?'

'The risk of not having surgery may be greater,' Ella said gently. 'I'll talk you both through any associated risks soon but you're actually at the safest stage of pregnancy to be having surgery. The risk of a miscarriage is higher in the first trimester and it gets technically a bit more complicated when the baby's bigger in the third trimester. We'll do the investigation laparoscopically and, if surgery is needed, we'll try and do that without having to open up your tummy, which means you'll have less likelihood of blood loss and a reduced need for medications, which is better for both of you.' Ella could see that Beth and her mother needed a bit of time to get over the shock of hearing that surgery might be needed. They also needed any reassurance she could give them at this point. 'You heard your baby's heartbeat, yes?'

Beth nodded, her face twisted with both pain and fear.

'He's not in any distress at the moment and that's a good sign.' Ella squeezed Beth's hand. 'We're going to look after you both, but we need to find out what's going on because you may be bleeding internally and we need to find out why and fix it.'

She caught Logan's gaze again then and she knew he would see a plea in her eyes. It wasn't that she wanted him to take over this case. What she wanted was for them to work together on it. The way they had for Lauren with her ruptured uterus and Iona with her dramatic surgery right here in this emergency department. They were a good team and Ella knew they were equally invested in keeping both a mother and her baby safe. More than a good team. Ella found this man inspirational in her professional arena and having his calm presence by her side gave her a confidence that was…empowering?

Together, they could tackle anything and Ella was far more likely to believe that they could win any medical battle. It was as simple as that.

He didn't need to nod. She could see that he understood. 'I'll let the guys here know I'm not going to make the meeting,' he told Ella. 'I'll also give Geoff, one of our general surgeons, an urgent call and get a theatre on standby while you go through the consent process with Beth.'

'Thank you.' Ella needed to get wide bore IV access in place for potential fluid resuscitation if Beth's blood pressure really crashed and she would also need a Foley catheter in preparation for surgery. They were going to be busy for the next little while but she gave no sign of being stressed as she gently wiped the ultrasound gel off Beth's distended abdomen. 'There you go,' she said. 'Dr Walsh is our head of department here at Queen's and he's on the case. You're in the best hands possible.'

* * *

Any doubts that he might have created difficulties in his working life by sleeping with Ella had been dispelled the moment Logan's path had crossed with Ella's on the ward yesterday.

Being in Theatre with her while she demonstrated her competence in manipulating laparoscopic instruments to try and discover the cause of their patient's abdominal pain made him very happy that he didn't need to avoid working closely with Ella because this was…impressive, that was what it was.

Logan had been more than happy to simply observe Ella's work, right from the first small incision below Beth's belly button to allow insertion of the first trochar that was used to infuse the gas to inflate the abdomen and the insertion of the laparascope with its bright light and video camera that sent the images onto the screen for the surgeons.

He could see what Ella could see and when her gaze flicked up to catch his for a heartbeat he knew exactly what she was thinking. While this wasn't an unheard-of complication in pregnancy, it was rare enough to qualify as a zebra and not a horse. This wasn't acute appendicitis or any of the other differential diagnoses that had sprung to mind initially.

'It's a heterotopic pregnancy with a ruptured ectopic,' Ella said for the benefit of the rest of the surgical team. 'It looks as though we'll need to do a total salpingectomy and remove this fallopian tube.'

Logan agreed. Beth had, in fact, become pregnant with twins and it was a heterotopic pregnancy because one of the implantations had happened where it should, in the uterus, but the other had become stuck and implanted itself in one of the fallopian tubes. The gestation of the healthy baby in the womb shouldn't be affected but the ectopic pregnancy was not viable and had to be removed before it endangered the mother's life. It was obstetric surgery and Logan was quite confident that Ella was more than capable to be the person performing it.

He assisted Ella to insert more trochars for both a left and right port on the side of Beth's abdomen. He watched the screen as she suctioned blood from the area around the affected fallopian tube.

'That's a litre of blood loss so far,' he noted. 'Do you want to start some blood products? Packed red cells?'

'Yes. Thank you.' Ella took a moment to glance at the screen with the display of the continuous monitoring of their patient's blood pressure, oxygen saturation and heart rate and rhythm. The anaesthetist gave her a reassuring nod.

'All good.'

Logan could see, on screen, the deft way Ella manipulated her instruments—graspers to hold tissue and to cauterise and cut the fallopian tube to stop the bleeding and remove the mass and a bag with purse strings to contain and then remove it. And he could see by looking at her face how intense her focus was. Somewhere in the back of his mind any doubts he might have had about it ever being difficult to work with Ella due to anything related to their personal lives evaporated. She might be far more involved with her patients on an emotional level than he ever became but she was as capable as he was himself of keeping enough distance not to let it affect her professional judgement.

Her patients were safe.

He was safe...

They did an intraoperative ultrasound to check on the condition of the baby in Beth's uterus and they checked again at the end of the procedure. Logan excused himself as Beth was transferred to the recovery suite.

'Everything's looking great,' he said to Ella quietly. 'Good job.'

'Thanks for being here,' she responded. 'I wasn't at all sure what we were going to find.'

'It was a pleasure,' Logan said. And he meant it. 'But I'd better get on with my day. I'm two meetings behind already and I've got my own theatre list. It might be a long day.'

'In that case, I think it must be my turn to provide dinner.' Ella's voice was quiet enough not be overheard but, even if it had been, it was casual enough for any hidden meaning to be missed unless you knew what had happened the last time they had had dinner together.

Ella knew.

Logan knew.

And the flick of a glance they shared as Ella stripped off her gloves and followed her patient out of Theatre made it crystal-clear that they both knew it was going to happen again.

Ella chose Mexican takeaway for their dinner and she had extra spice added to their tacos and burritos and quesadillas but it was never going to be able to compete with the heat that seemed to ignite in an instant between herself and Logan Walsh.

The food had been waiting on Ella's kitchen bench to be reheated because she had no idea what time Logan would get away from work and all it took for that meal to be totally forgotten was the knock on her door just after nine p.m. When she opened the door to see the look in Logan's eyes Ella was already lost in the moment.

He was kissing her even as he dropped his bag by the door and pushed it shut. Off balance, Ella needed the support of the wall at her back so that she could raise her arms to wrap them around Logan's neck but he caught her hands and held them above her head and kissed her so thoroughly that her head was spinning by the time she had a chance to catch her breath.

'I should go home,' he said, sounding out of breath himself. 'It's been a long day and I need a shower.'

'Don't go…' When she ran her tongue over her bottom lip Ella could still taste him. 'I've got a shower…'

He was watching her mouth. And then he lifted his gaze and Ella had never felt less hungry for food in her life. Seconds later, they were in the small bathroom of her apartment, which wasn't built for two people using it at the same time so it meant getting really close as they undressed each other, and they were skin to skin when they got in under the rain of hot water. And then there was a slippery bar of soap and the foam of shampoo and more kissing. There was laughter and murmurs of pleasure and encouragement and… and it was the best sex Ella had ever experienced in her life.

Until they wrapped themselves in towels and went to her bed and did it all over again and that was slow and tender and…

…and Ella knew she was beginning to fall in love with a man who could be so distant and calmly professional on one hand and have the ability to make love like *this* on the other. He was an intense, super intelligent and passionate man but he was also more controlled than anyone she'd ever met and that gave him an air of mystery that was more than simply intriguing. It was compelling…

She could feel his heart beating strongly and swiftly under her cheek as she nestled in his arms.

'Where did you learn to be this good in bed?' she asked.

Logan gave a grunt of laughter. 'I could ask you the same thing.'

'Hey… I'm well out of practice. It's been quite a while for me.'

'Same…' But there was a gleam in Logan's eyes. 'I'll look forward to you getting your mojo back,' he said. 'I'll just have to hope I can keep up.'

Ella lifted herself onto one elbow so that she could reach his lips with her own. 'I have every confidence in your ability,' she told him. 'And, seeing as we've got a limited shelf life, we should probably make the most of it, don't you think?'

For a long, long moment, Logan held her gaze silently and Ella's heart skipped a beat. Was he going to tell her that this couldn't happen again? That he never let people into his life far enough to throw caution to the winds and indulge in a passionate affair?

This wasn't something Ella had ever done before in her life either, but it was in this moment that she realised just how much she wanted to spend the remainder of her time in Aberdeen with Logan. It wasn't only because of the amazing sexual connection they'd discovered with each other. She really wanted to get to know him. To understand what had made him into the person he was today—a man who was capable of so much passion and yet he'd chosen to funnel it almost entirely into his career. Wasn't he lonely, at least sometimes?

She didn't believe that he lived alone and had no significant relationships outside of work purely in order not to dilute that focus because she could sense something much bigger had been responsible for shaping his ability to distance himself and be content to be alone. Something traumatic enough to make Logan hide a significant part of who he was. Enough to create a barrier that Ella knew she might never be able to breach, but that wasn't enough to push her away. If anything, it was making her feel even more drawn to him.

You couldn't fall in love with someone unless the connection was on a much deeper level than just sex. You had to care about them. A lot. And if you cared about someone that much it was only to be expected that you would want to understand what might be holding them back from being as happy as they deserved to be.

Ella had just reminded them both that they only had a limited amount of time to be together and that they should make the most of it, but now she was holding her breath, wondering if she'd pushed a little too hard against that barrier and she'd never get an opportunity to understand why it was there in the first place—or think about whether she might be able to contribute more than just a memorable physical fling to Logan's life.

What if she could help him loosen that hold he had on his emotions and he realised that there was more to life than work? If he not only got persuaded to live in that bit of rural paradise he'd been inspired to purchase but shared it with someone he could love as much as they loved him?

It seemed as if Logan might be reading her thoughts because he was smiling, but when he spoke she realised that he had backed off into a safely distant place because he was speaking in the same tone he might have used to tell her about an interesting case he'd seen recently.

'I'm going up to Inverness in a week or so,' he said. 'To present an obstetric emergencies seminar. I'll leave Friday afternoon, do the seminar on Saturday and be back here by about eight p.m. Maybe you'd like to come with me if it fits in with your roster? It might be a good chance for you to find out everything you want to know about the course with a bit of sightseeing thrown in? We could come back over the Old Military Road, which is worth seeing if you've never driven it. Some people say it's one of the best roads in the UK.'

Ella drew in a breath. While it was disappointing that Logan had retreated from the closeness that had been there while they'd been making love, she was relieved to discover she hadn't pushed too hard on that barrier after all. Logan wasn't running. Or, if he was, he was inviting her to go with him and she liked that. He was making it sound as if he wanted her company too, by throwing in the bonus of some sightseeing. It was possible she might be able to find out as much about Logan as the course's clinical content but, if not, it would be a longer time in his company than she had had so far and there was no way she could turn that down. Not with the strength of that pull she could feel towards him.

But she kept her response light. Affirmative but casual. No big deal. No pushing of any boundaries involved.

'Sure,' she said. 'Sounds great... I'm in.'

CHAPTER EIGHT

LOGAN COULDN'T REMEMBER exactly when he'd started his programme of advanced training and refresher courses for medical professionals who were likely to have anything to do with pregnant women and childbirth but it was quite a few years ago now.

Initially, he'd worked with the local ambulance service, midwives and general practitioners who still offered obstetric services, but word had spread and he'd started getting invitations to work with other centres that offered a convenient hub for remote areas and he'd been more than happy to fit those commitments into his schedule. He sometimes got flown to cities all over the United Kingdom, but he particularly enjoyed being able to pack what he needed into the spacious hatch of his vehicle and drive off to explore his own backyard. His roots were very firmly in Scottish soil and he appreciated the often breathtaking landscape it offered.

He liked the break in his normal routine too. Ella might lose herself in dreaming up and sketching house restorations and renovations but this was his 'time out', even though it was still so closely related to his day-to-day work. And meeting new like-minded people who shared his vision in making childbirth as safe as possible was the closest thing Logan had to a social life, in fact. It was never a hardship travelling to parts of Scotland that he didn't know so well, but these days he was starting to revisit many of them. He knew they were heading into Forres now without needing any signposts.

'That's Nelson's Tower you can see on the hill over there. And there's the Witches Stone I stopped to have a look at once. I won't horrify you with the gory details of that grim bit of history.'

'I'll look it up myself,' Ella warned. 'I love everything about Scotland. The history and some of the countryside might be grim but it's got a wildness that's unique.'

Logan loved his homeland too, but enjoying its scenery and people and the snippets of history that he discovered was a bonus. He wasn't travelling around to have fun, after all. This was what he was most passionate about and what had become his personal mission in life. Teaching skills and giving people the confidence to handle emergencies because, even if it helped to save one life, it was worth putting all this time and effort into. As he'd said to Ella, the fact that the paramedics who'd been called to that cardiac arrest case they'd done the resuscitative hysterotomy on had recently done a course and were up-to-date with how to modify CPR for a pregnant patient could have made the crucial difference to the outcome for both mother and baby.

And that reminded him…

'She's doing really well,' he told Ella. 'Our mother who had the cardiac arrest.'

'Iona?' Ella looked up from the sketch pad on her lap that she'd gone back to working on as they left the town behind. 'I know… I went to visit her this morning and she and Finlay were having their first go at breastfeeding.'

'Successful?'

'He didn't quite manage to latch on properly but it's early days and it's a big step forward. He's doing well with bottle feeding and it was just wonderful to see him being held by his mum. Iona was crying happy tears.

Oh, and he passed his hearing test this week too, and he's started to track things visually. I'm sure he's watching me when I go to visit him now.'

Logan was starting to regret mentioning the case. Ella didn't care that she got too involved with patients, did she? She made it sound as if it was quite okay for her to still be visiting a baby every day whose mother wasn't even her patient. She was clearly revelling in every positive step of the journey Iona and her family were embarked on. Logan shook his head.

'Are you still visiting him every day?'

'If I can. I love seeing his progress.'

Logan didn't need to turn his head. He could hear the smile in Ella's voice.

'I told him I'd try and find a toy Loch Ness monster for him while I'm away this weekend,' she said.

Logan did turn his head this time. 'I don't know how you do it,' he said.

'Do what?'

'Get so involved with the patients you treat—and their families. I mean, it's fine if a case goes well but how do you cope with the ones that don't go well when you get that close? I've seen people having to walk away from the careers they loved because they can't protect themselves from the downside of a tragedy they feel too connected with.'

'I guess it's a matter of balance,' Ella said thoughtfully, after a short silence. 'Protecting yourself from not feeling the pain of a distressing case means that you're not feeling the joy of the majority of our cases and isn't that what makes this the best career in the world? Helping babies get born...helping families get created?'

'I agree that it's a matter of balance.' Logan nodded. 'But you can't let the pendulum swing too far in either direction—whether it's the happy side or the painful one. If it swings too far, that's when things can get out of control. And when you can make bad decisions.'

'My pendulum probably does swing a bit more than yours,' Ella admitted. 'But I never get *too* involved. I can't, because I'm never in one place for long enough so there's no danger of getting too attached—to people or places. That would definitely do my head in when I had to move on.'

'Because your freedom is everything.' Logan's words were no more than a thinking aloud kind of murmur but Ella obviously heard him.

'And adventures,' she said firmly. 'I do love an adventure.' She was peering ahead at a signpost they were approaching. 'I've never been to Nairn,' she said. 'Do you know anything about it?'

'I believe it's an old fishing port and a seaside resort. We've got time for a quick look if you like.'

'Ooh, yes, please. I haven't been near a beach since I was in California. I'm missing waves.'

If Ella was trying to change the subject of their conversation, that smile was an encouragement that Logan couldn't refuse. Maybe these courses weren't intended to be fun, but he'd known deep down that having Ella's company would make things very different and mixing fun with work wasn't necessarily a bad thing, was it?

He smiled back. 'I might even buy you an ice cream if you behave yourself.'

It was like being on a real date with Logan Walsh for the first time.

They found ice creams at a beach café that advertised interesting flavours like cinnamon basil and Ella's choice of chocolate liquorice. She rolled her eyes when Logan went for a boringly safe vanilla but refrained from teasing him. They wandered off to admire the ornate Victorian era bandstand with its cast-iron finials and steeply curved roof while they ate them and then walked hand in hand on the beach and let the fresh sea breeze ruffle their hair and the waves break and roll so close they had to jump out of the way to keep their feet dry. It wasn't far to Inverness after that and daylight was fading so they stopped by a fish and chip shop near the river and sat on the bench in the shadow of the castle eating fish dinners with little wooden forks.

Ella wanted to keep the feeling of being on a date, even though she knew this was a work-related trip, so she did her best to entertain Logan with stories that had nothing to do with work and counted it a win when he snorted with amusement hearing about the alpacas that spat all over her in Peru and then laughed out loud at her description of what her triplet brothers looked like when they'd stolen their mother's nail scissors and given each other haircuts when they were about three years old.

It was the first time she'd heard Logan really laugh and it gave Ella a squeeze in her chest that was pure happiness.

She realised it would be the first time they would actually sleep in the same bed too, when they checked into a bed and breakfast establishment in the attic of a lovely old sandstone villa. Even though Ella knew they had a very early start the next morning, to set up the training room in a local hospital for the seminar, she wanted to stay awake and enjoy the prospect of drifting off to sleep in Logan's arms after their lovemaking, knowing that he would still be there beside her when she woke up in the morning.

And in that final moment, hanging in that misty space between thinking and dreaming, Ella remembered what she'd said to Logan in the car about being in no danger of getting too involved with any person or place because she never stayed anywhere long enough for it to become an issue. She couldn't have been in control of where her thoughts were drifting, however, because for a distinct moment she could imagine being with just one person. Settling down in just one place, even. Being so much in love with someone that it would be worthwhile giving up the freedom to go wherever she wanted to go in the world and have whatever adventures took her fancy.

Was she more than halfway towards being that much in love with Logan?

If she was, there was no point in worrying about giving up her freedom yet or starting to think about what it might be like to put down roots in one place because Logan was just as determined to protect his own version of freedom as she'd been over the last few years. He was never going to let his emotional pendulum swing far enough to distract him from his work and he wasn't about to include anyone else in his personal life.

And that was a good thing, even if it meant that Logan was sacrificing what many would think of as being one of the most important aspects of life. Ella had experienced the calm confidence that Logan's ability to keep his distance could bring to the way he handled an emergency and if she was a patient she would want someone exactly like that to be in charge.

Her thoughts circled back once more to that small epiphany as she finally fell asleep—that maybe she would consider settling down one day if she met the 'right' person—but this time she let the thought evaporate without taking any further notice. 'One day' was too far in the future to see and there was no reason at all to let it interfere with the present. It was rather nice, though, to think that she might find a partner who could add a permanent extra dimension to her personal life. The way Logan could when it came to her professional life?

She snuggled closer to the person she was with. While it wasn't an unpleasant idea that she might find that perfect partner in the future, she didn't need the 'right' one yet. She could enjoy the 'right now' person she had been lucky enough to meet.

This had to be the best group of medical professionals that Logan had ever had the pleasure of teaching. There were twenty people ranging in age from mid-twenties to late-fifties and they had come from all over some of the most northern areas of Scotland and as far east as Skye. They were engaged with the subject matter and eager to either learn new skills or practise the ones they already had because they might only have to deal with an obstetric emergency once in a blue moon and it was easy to forget how to do something you didn't do on a regular basis.

It wasn't the first time Logan had brought an assistant with him to help run the seminar, but this was Ella and he might have known it would be different.

The first session of this intense one-day course, after introductions and an icebreaker, was the subject of breech births.

'Because they account for three to four percent of all full-term pregnancies so you're likely to encounter one at some point. They can happen suddenly, especially if the baby is premature and it hasn't had the chance to turn itself around, and that can also mean it's quite likely to happen away from a nice, controlled hospital setting.'

Logan had one hip perched on the corner of the desk at the front of the room, with a laser pointer in his hand as he opened up an audio-visual presentation on the big screen that had been lowered over a blackboard. Ella was standing on the other side of the classroom and was holding one of the infant manikins that went with the lower torso models used to practise delivery techniques.

The first slide had images of babies in various breech positions within the uterus.

'A frank breech is what we prefer to deal with, where the baby's bottom presents first with the legs straight up in front of the body and the feet near the head.'

Ella held the soft manikin baby in front of her and bent its legs straight up.

'A complete breech is where both the hips and knees are flexed so that it looks as though the baby is sitting cross-legged and a footling breech is where one or both feet will deliver first.'

Maybe it was the look of dismay on Ella's face as she let one of the manikin's legs dangle that led to the ripple of laughter that ran through the classroom. It could have been a distraction from what was actually a very serious topic to cover but Logan could feel a corner of his own mouth curling upwards.

Perhaps this was why it felt like the best group of participants he'd ever had? Because there was a hint of something lighter in the atmosphere than Logan had encountered before? It felt like a good thing. Surely if people were relaxed and comfortable they would learn more easily and wouldn't hesitate to ask questions if there was something they needed more clarification on?

It wasn't until he'd divided the room up into five groups of four people, each with a table and manikins and a work sheet to practise delivery techniques for type of breech presentation, that Logan could pinpoint what was so different about today's course.

He'd seen the way Ella could connect with people. He could remember the very first patient she had seen at Queen's as they'd rushed her off to Theatre. The young mother was in trouble. Despite being in agonising pain and frightened, she had made a heartfelt plea.

'But I want Ella to look after me...'

And then there'd been Iona's husband and the way he'd bonded with Ella as the doctor who understood exactly the overwhelming emotions he was dealing with as his wife was still fighting for her life and his tiny baby was doing the same thing in a very different part of the hospital.

Somehow, Ella had connected with twenty people she'd never met before without even trying and there was a buzz in the room that was energising for both the instructor and the people here to learn. Having Ella with him not only made everything different, Logan thought, it made it a whole lot better.

And how much more fun had the journey been to get here in the first place? He might have been tempted enough in the past to visit the intriguing Witches Stone but he would never have stopped to eat ice cream and walk on a beach. Or eat fish and chips sitting by a river with a castle as a backdrop. It was, quite frankly, life-changing to be around Ella Grisham and she was right—it wasn't going to be for very long so they needed to make the most of it.

'When you've got Ella at your station...' Logan raised his voice so that everybody could hear him. 'Get her to show you how to deal with entrapment. I watched her deliver a breech baby with a nuchal arm very recently and I'm sure she'll walk you through it better than I can.'

She was smiling at him as he turned back to the group he was working with and, for a fleeting moment, he held that eye contact. Because it felt good. Because he was really enjoying himself? A young paramedic was halfway through a practice run of a breech delivery, with both legs of the baby already born.

'Grasp the baby so that your thumbs are over the baby's hips,' Logan advised. 'If you hold any higher than that, there's some risk of injury to the kidneys and abdominal organs. Wrapping a towel around the baby will improve your grip and lessen the need for too much pressure. If you've got someone to help, get them to apply suprapubic pressure to keep the head flexed.'

He glanced back at the table where Ella was a minute or two later and he could hear her answering a question about freeing a trapped arm.

'I'm not going to hurt the baby, am I?'

'There are some risks,' Ella told them. 'It's possible to cause fractures or dislocations to the shoulder, collarbone or humerus so be as gentle as you can, but remember...broken bones will heal. If the baby stays trapped it will end in a fatality and that's exactly why you're here today, isn't it? To try and make sure you can avoid having a case that might haunt you for the rest of your life?'

Logan turned back to his own student. 'That's great,' he encouraged the paramedic. 'Don't raise the baby above the horizontal axis until you can see the mouth and nose,' he added. 'That way, you'll avoid hyperextension and the risk of a spinal injury. Okay... who's next?'

He needed to move things along because they still had a lot to cover before the lunch break, including cord prolapse and shoulder dystocia, but there was something else vying for attention at the back of Logan's head.

Something Ella had said about this being the best career in the world. About letting yourself experience the joy of it going well. Had he ever done that? Or was relief the only emotion he allowed himself to feel at the end of a well-managed birth?

He envied that easy connection she could find with people. He also envied the way she could feel joy to such an extent that it over-flowed and made her dance in a corridor. Was he even capable of letting his emotional pendulum swing a little further on that spectrum? And, if he did, would he feel joy again?

Maybe the real question was whether he was brave enough to try…

They packed up all the manikins and other teaching aids, collected leftover handouts and tidied the seminar room with participants still lingering to say how much they'd enjoyed the course and how much they'd learned.

'Can you guys stay for a while?' The young paramedic Logan had worked with on the breech delivery practical work seemed the most reluctant to leave but it was Ella he was speaking to. 'Some of us are going out to dinner together and there's a great bar not far away which always has a live band and good music on a Saturday night. Do you like dancing, Ella?'

Ella caught a glance from Logan, who was shutting down his laptop at the desk. She knew perfectly well that he was thinking about seeing her dancing in the hospital corridor that evening and she felt a flush of warmth reach her cheeks. Because it was still a slightly embarrassing thing for him to have witnessed? Or was it that she liked the fact that he was thinking about it at all? It was another personal secret—like the joke about hitting on each other...

'I do...' Ella hurriedly stuffed a silicone pelvis and abdomen into its protective cover. 'But we have to head straight back to Aberdeen, don't we, Logan?'

'We do. Sorry, mate.' Logan didn't sound sorry. 'Ella's working tomorrow and I'm on first call so we need to be back in Aberdeen tonight. And we're going to drive back over the Old Military Road so we need what's left of the daylight for that. There wouldn't be much point in going that way if we can't see the views.'

'No worries.' The paramedic shrugged and

then winked at Ella. 'It was worth a try. Let me help you carry some of this gear out to your car.'

If Ella had wanted immersion in some of the wildest and most beautiful of Scottish landscapes, this road through the Cairngorms would have been her first choice. They passed isolated farmhouses—one even advertising that it was a B&B—along a rollercoaster of hills and dips, twisty curves and stunning views across farmland and mountains. Startled deer ran away from them across endless bare stretches of grassland and there was even a touch of snow on the highest pass.

'I can imagine people loving a stay at that B&B to get totally away from it all,' Ella said. 'And it must be gorgeous up here when it really snows, but the road probably has to close, yes?'

'Not often,' Logan responded. 'But it is one of the first British roads that will close during a snowstorm. It gets a bit dangerous.'

'I'll bet. I'm glad we can keep going. I love it, but I'll be happy to be a bit closer to home before it gets dark.'

'Speaking of which, if there's still any light

when we're going past the barn, do you mind if we stop for a few minutes?'

'Not at all. I'd love to see it again. It's all very well doing sketches from photos but the feeling of the place isn't the same.'

'I'd love a copy of some of your sketches, if that's okay. I spoke to the estate agent that sold me the place and told him what you were doing and he thought it might really help to get a fast sale. He also wants me to get a bit of a tidy-up done, so I want to have a look and see how much work it would be. It might be a lot quicker to hire some grass-cutting equipment and do it myself on my next day off.'

Ella could feel her heart sinking. She didn't want Logan to sell that magical old barn with its pixie house and pond and resident ducks. She had been enjoying working on her sketches because she was hoping he might change his mind. That she might be sketching a vision of his own—happy—future.

But he was still intent on selling it.

And it wasn't any of her business anyway. Because she wouldn't be here.

Her heart sank a little further. Ella leaned her head back and closed her eyes.

'You okay, El?'

It wasn't just that he'd used a diminutive of

her name that no one else ever had. It was the very genuine concern in Logan's voice that was threatening to undo Ella. The idea that he really *cared* about her?

Even if he did, it wouldn't change anything. He was going to sell the barn and make sure that nothing distracted him from the only focus he wanted in his life, which had nothing to do with property or personal relationships. And a meaningful relationship wasn't something that Ella wanted anyway, so why on earth was she feeling this odd sense of, what was it…disappointment?

A hint of heartbreak, even?

Random thoughts that she might be ready to settle in one place, with one person, needed squashing. A relationship would tie her down and there would be the expectation of starting a family and she'd already spent too much of her life being a surrogate mother.

Ella was all too aware of how easy it was to sacrifice—or be *expected* to sacrifice—personal desires or even needs because of how much you loved the babies in your life. This was *her* time now. She got all the time with babies anyone could wish for in her working life and, best of all, she got to hand them to their mothers for all the hard work. Given how popular all her brothers were with women, no doubt they'd be producing their own offspring before long too. Ella could imagine herself as the fun auntie who was a part of all their lives but had an important job she was very, very good at as well.

She could be exactly the person she wanted to be.

But who was that again? The confidence with which Ella had always imagined her future self seemed to have become blurry around the edges—as if she wasn't quite so sure about the outline of that image any longer.

'I'm fine,' she said without opening her eyes. 'Just a bit tired.'

She did look a bit tired.

Logan only stopped briefly at the barn.

'Where on earth would I start?' he wondered aloud. 'The grass is probably high enough to stop someone wanting to even get out of their car and this isn't the best side of the barn to be looking at, is it?'

'You could cut a path through the grass, leading around to the other side. It would be an invitation that most people wouldn't be able to resist.'

'That's a great idea.'

'I'm full of them.' Ella smiled but didn't get out of the car to follow Logan as he went to see if there were any obstacles to creating that path.

There didn't seem to be. And if he focused on clearing the area between the ancient building and the pond at the end of the path from the lane, it should be enough to encourage any potential buyers to stand in the perfect spot to imagine the outdoor courtyard in Ella's sketches, with the big windows in the wall of the barn and the pixie house opened up enough to make a romantic little summer house. He was going to need to hire a commercial grade grass trimmer and lawnmower and some loppers, hedge clippers and a pruning saw might be a good idea as well, to trim back some of the ivy scrambling over stone walls and to shape the trailing branches of the weeping willow beside the pond.

'Doable.' He nodded as he got back into his car. 'But still a big day's work.' He glanced at Ella's face as he started the engine again. Was she okay? Was it his imagination or did she look a bit pale? Sad, even…?

'Are you any good with a grass trimmer or lawnmower?' he asked lightly. He lowered his voice into a deliberately OTT sexy drawl. 'If you came to help me, I promise I'd make it worth your while.'

That made her laugh. 'Might be good practice,' she said. 'Being good with machinery might look good on my CV, and who knows what extra skills I'll need in Australia? Apparently the hospital I'm going to works with the flying doctor service for anything to do with obs and gynae. I might need to learn something about planes as well. Imagine if we break down somewhere in the outback?'

Logan could imagine Ella in the Australian outback. She was wearing a ripped pair of jeans, cowboy boots and a loose white shirt with the sleeves rolled up. Her long hair was hanging down her back in a braid from beneath one of those hats with the corks dangling around the brim. She looked…ultimately desirable… Not purely in a sexual way either. She was great company—as sharp as a tack and as warm and generous as anybody you could hope to meet. A friend as well as an amazing lover.

He was going to miss her when she moved on, that was for sure.

'That sounds like something that will be right up your alley,' he told her. 'An exciting job, a country that's renowned for the freedom it offers and so many adventures you won't be able to keep up with them all. What more could you possibly want?'

Ella laughed again, and this time it seemed to dispel some of that weariness. 'Nothing,' she agreed. She sounded almost cheerful now. 'Nothing at all.'

CHAPTER NINE

WHEN ELLA HAD applied for this locum position at the Queen Mother's Maternity Hospital in Aberdeen she had been hoping she would be able to become a part of the team headed by Logan Walsh that provided education and responded to emergency obstetric cases.

It had never occurred to her that she might need to activate a call to the response team herself but here she was, in the car park of the closest shopping centre to the hospital that had a supermarket, beside a car with an obviously pregnant woman sitting sideways behind the steering wheel with her legs hanging outside. A woman who was crying in agony and currently vomiting uncontrollably.

'Are you having contractions?' Ella asked. 'Have your waters broken? Are you bleeding?'

'No-o.' The woman shook her head. 'Oh, God…it really hurts. And I feel *so* sick…'

'How far along are you?'

'Almost thirty-three weeks.'

Ella was trying to take her pulse but she couldn't feel one in the woman's wrist, which meant that her blood pressure might be way too low.

'My name's Ella,' she said. 'I'm an obstetrician at Queen's.'

'That's where I'm supposed to go for my Caesarean.'

'You're having an elective Caesarean?' Ella knew this meant there had to be known complications of some kind with this pregnancy. 'Okay…hang on. I'm going to get an ambulance on the way for you and then I'll ask you some more questions.'

She dialled the emergency phone number and gave her location. When she told the call taker that she was a doctor and this was an obstetric emergency the dispatcher said she was giving the call the highest priority.

'I'll activate the Obstetric Emergency Response Team as well. They'll be with you as soon as possible.'

It took long enough for the ambulance to arrive for Ella to have acquired a lot more information. It wasn't really a surprise that Logan had been available to join the ambulance crew—this was the kind of thing he lived for, wasn't it? Logan, however, was very surprised when he jumped out of the back of the ambulance.

'Ella? What on earth are you doing here?'

It was Ella's day off. She had come, by bus, to this supermarket with a list of the things she needed because she wanted to cook dinner for Logan instead of sharing a takeaway meal like they usually did. Her list included fillet steak and mushrooms, the ingredients to make a potato gratin and a reminder to choose all her favourite salad items. She had been intending to impress him. And then seduce him. Or let him seduce her—whichever came first... But any explanation of what she was doing here and why merely flashed through the back of her head with a whiff of wry amusement and then vanished into thin air.

'This is Gemma McKay,' she told him. 'Thirty-three weeks pregnant. Sudden onset of severe, ten out of ten, abdominal pain about half an hour ago. She's unable to move and her abdomen is rigid and extremely tender. No contractions and no observable bleeding but her radial pulse is absent. She's been vomiting frequently.'

'I know Gemma.' Logan was still sounding surprised as he crouched down in front of the woman. 'I'm Logan Walsh. I think I did your first Caesarean, didn't I? When you'd gone a couple of weeks over your due date and the baby wasn't happy?'

'Oh...' Gemma raised her face. 'Yes... I'm so happy to see you, Dr Walsh.' Her face crumpled into lines of pain. 'Something's going really horribly wrong this time...'

'Let's get you into the ambulance and take you into hospital. We'll be able to take much better care of you when we're not in a car park.'

The ambulance crew helped get Gemma onto a stretcher and into the back of the ambulance. Ella shut the door of her car and locked it, climbing into the ambulance to put Gemma's handbag somewhere safe.

'I've put your car keys in your bag,' she said. 'Your phone's in there too.'

'I need to call my mum.' Gemma was having a blood pressure cuff wrapped around her arm, an oxygen saturation probe clipped to her finger and Logan had his hands very gently on her abdomen but it was still making her grimace. She kept her gaze on Ella, however. 'Mum'll need to pick Timmy up from childcare for me. His dad doesn't finish work till six o'clock and he'll be on the road anyway.'

'Maybe I can do that for you.' Ella found Gemma's phone.

'BP's fifty-six over forty,' the paramedic in the back with Logan reported. 'Heart rate one-one-four. Her temperature's normal. Oxygen saturation a hundred percent on air.'

Logan sounded remarkably calm given that Gemma's blood pressure was dangerously low. No wonder she was feeling so sick.

'Let's get an IV in and some fluids up,' was all he said. 'And I think we should get moving very soon. Ella, could you ride with us? I might need you...'

Of course she could. If Logan thought he might need assistance he must be worried that Gemma's condition was serious and Ella was prepared for anything. She made a quick call to Gemma's mother, who was happy to pick up her grandson, as Logan unrolled an IV kit and put a tourniquet around Gemma's arm.

'Try and keep really still for me,' he said. 'We need to get a line in and give you some fluids but your blood pressure's very low so your veins might not want to cooperate.'

The paramedic in the driver's seat of the ambulance was leaning to look into the cabin. 'Want to get moving, Doc?'

'No. Wait a sec.' Logan was carefully inserting a needle under the skin, clearly searching for the antecubital vein which would be much easier to access than anything smaller but Ella could see how difficult it was, which suggested that Gemma's veins were on the point of collapsing.

A tiny flash of blood in the cannula chamber showed that Logan had found the vein but it was at that moment that Gemma suddenly moved.

'I'm going to be sick...'

Logan shook his head and took the needle out of her arm as she jerked. The paramedic held a container for Gemma and supported her head. Logan straightened to meet Ella's gaze.

'Blood pressure this low with no evidence of bleeding and vomiting that could be due to vagal stimulation makes me think this is neurogenic rather than hypovolaemic shock.'

Any shock, with the subsequent shutdown of organs due to insufficient oxygen, was dangerous. Fluid resuscitation was the first response and it was needed urgently.

'Intraosseous access?'

Logan nodded. 'We need to get moving and it'll be quicker than anything else. Could you set up the fluids and giving set?'

'Sure.' Ella opened a glass-fronted overhead cupboard where she could see the units of saline were stored. As she opened packs to hang the bag and attach the tubing set before running some fluid through the line to get rid of any air bubbles, she could see how swiftly Logan was working beside her.

Gemma was still in the throes of vomiting and barely heard Logan explaining what was happening as he opened the IO kit. He felt for the markers below her knee, attached the needle to the drill and it was through the skin and into the bone marrow space of her tibia within seconds. Ella could see the concentration on his face and for a split second she remembered how intimidated she'd been on that first meeting, when he'd burst into the delivery room and stood there glaring at her. She knew now that it was simply an expression of how important what he was doing was.

How much he cared.

And she loved him for that. She trusted him completely as well. There was no one she would rather be working with.

Logan secured the port with a dressing and attached tubing with a syringe on the end that he used to flush the line. Ella could hand him the end of the tubing in her hand to replace the syringe and adjusted the drip rate to increase the speed of the infusion.

'We're good to go,' Logan said. 'We'll get some pain relief on board while we travel.'

The engine was already running and lights and the siren were activated to get them to the hospital as quickly as possible, but Ella was happy to see that Gemma's blood pressure had already risen a little with the fluids she was receiving. Logan called ahead to alert the emergency department of their arrival and to request Gemma's medical records. She was under the care of another obstetrician for this pregnancy so he hadn't had anything to do with her since her Caesarean more than three years ago.

A resuscitation area had been cleared for them and one of the ED consultants had been busy getting ready for their arrival.

'We've got a CTG machine here and portable ultrasound. We've tried to contact her obstetrician but he's unavailable. We have got her records and she had an antenatal visit last week.'

'And…?'

'Nothing of concern noted. She'd been getting some pain during the night and when she rested in the afternoons but it stopped when she changed position and moved. She has a low lying anterior placenta but an elective C-section without a trial of labour had been the preferred option from the start after the problems Gemma had last time.'

Ella was getting ready to place the foetal monitoring electrodes on Gemma's abdomen as soon as Logan finished the ultrasound examination. He squeezed gel onto her skin and then touched the transducer to her skin.

'Ow…' Gemma burst into tears. 'That hurts…'

Ella took hold of her hand. 'Sorry, sweetheart, I know it's painful. We'll be able to give you something more for that pain as soon as we get an idea of what's going on.'

'I'm scared…' Gemma sobbed.

Logan moved the transducer, his gaze fixed on the screen. 'I can see your baby's heart,' he told Gemma. 'It's moving well. He's not too bothered by whatever's going on in there.'

'It's a girl…'

'Is it?' Ella squeezed her hand again.

'Timmy must be excited about getting a little sister.'

'I can't see any evidence of bleeding,' Logan said. 'And the previous scar tissue is intact. Baby's in a transverse lie. And there's the placenta.' He turned to the ED consultant. 'It's posterior. Didn't the notes say it was anterior?'

'They did. Probably a typo.'

'Hmm...'

Logan had finished the ultrasound examination and Ella wiped the gel off Gemma's skin and then attached the transducers for the CTG. The trace of uterine activity suggested an irritability, with low level contractions that weren't likely to be affecting the cervix. The baby's heart rate was initially a good rate of one hundred and forty but, even as Ella started printing a recording, it dropped to just over a hundred. It picked up and then dropped again, with no cessation of the uterine irritability, and the decision was made to take Gemma to Theatre for an emergency Caesarean.

Ella could have excused herself at that point because she wasn't actually on duty today. Except she couldn't, could she? She'd been the person who'd found Gemma in trouble and had been by her side ever since. There were no family members here to comfort and reassure her as she was taken to Theatre and Ella knew how frightened she had to be. She wasn't about to leave.

Besides… Logan had wanted her to come back to the hospital with him. Because he might need her. And just the possibility of being needed by Logan was an even more powerful reason to stay.

'There's something about you, Ella…' Logan was standing beside the wall of stainless-steel scrub sinks adjacent to the operating theatre they were preparing to enter. His hands and arms were soapy and he was using the nail brush to clean each fingernail, one at a time. 'You and zebras.'

'Oh?'

Ella had just begun to soap her skin. Her hair was tucked away under the disposable hat and her mouth and nose were covered with a mask so it was only her eyes that Logan could see—along with the movement of the tiny muscles around them that let him know she was smiling beneath that mask. It was more than just a smile, though. There was a warmth in her eyes that was only there because they'd become so close. A look that was for him alone?

Whatever… It kind of felt like they were holding hands…

Oh, man…he really was going to miss Ella when she moved on.

But what if she didn't?

'I forgot to tell you,' he said. 'Kirsty—the O&G consultant you're filling in for—has just put in her resignation. She's not coming back.'

Ella was opening the pack that contained the soap-impregnated nail brush. 'Really? Is she enjoying being a mother too much?'

'I suspect that's part of it, but her husband's got a new job. They'll be moving to Ireland before her maternity leave is finished.' He deliberately kept his tone light so that it wouldn't seem as if he was putting any pressure on Ella. 'I'll be advertising the permanent position straight away. I just thought I'd let you know in case…' he pulled in a breath as he put his hand under the tap, letting water stream down his arm to his elbow '…in case you're finding it good enough here to want to stay a bit longer?'

Ella seemed to be avoiding his gaze now, focused on finishing her nails. 'A permanent position is a whole different ball game to staying a bit longer,' she said. 'And I think Australia might have more adventures on offer.'

There was a moment's silence and then Ella's tone changed to one of amusement. Or was she trying to change the subject?

'No zebras at the bottom of the world, though. What did you mean when you said "you and zebras"?'

Logan was drying his hands. 'There are some cases that are so rare they're once-in-a-lifetime scenarios. I'm starting to think that Gemma might be one of them.'

There was nothing soft or personal about the eye contact this time. Ella was thinking only of their patient, who was currently in the hands of the anaesthetist and theatre team, being prepped for the emergency Caesarean. It eliminated any thoughts about trying to talk Ella into staying in Aberdeen as Logan also focused completely and…he was aware of a faint wash of relief as he did so. He didn't want to think about how much he was going to miss having Ella in his life. He didn't want to think about any implications of why he'd just encouraged her to stay either.

'What if that discrepancy in the position of the placenta wasn't a typo?' he continued.

'And that was the piece of the puzzle to add to what looks like hypovolaemic shock when there's no evidence of bleeding?'

Ella had just rinsed her arms and hands. She was holding them in front of her and they were dripping but she wasn't reaching for her sterile towel. 'A uterine torsion?' she breathed. 'I've never seen one.'

'Neither have I, but the early symptoms could fit.' Logan was thinking aloud as he put his gown on. 'She's had episodes of pain on rest that went away when she changed position and moved around. What if she was getting a partial torsion that resolved itself, until the gestation reached a point where it was too big for that to happen?'

'And if the uterus had turned to a hundred and eighty degrees, then the placenta would seem to be on the opposite side on ultrasound. Maybe there was no typo in the notes.'

'Exactly.' Logan was putting his gloves on now. Then he turned to let a theatre technician tie his gown.

Ella was catching up in her prep. She'd dried her hands and put her arms into the sleeves of her gown. It would only be seconds before she was also gloved and ready to enter Theatre. They were possibly about to face a surgical case that neither of them had any experience with and Logan was very happy that he had Ella as his assistant. He knew how good she was at her job and how well they worked together.

He led the way into Theatre, aware that, as a team, they were better than either of them would be on their own and that gave him a confidence that let him focus even more sharply. He was also aware of how rare it was to find a colleague like this.

It was a kind of zebra instead of a horse all by itself.

Ella knew Logan's suspicion was confirmed the moment they opened Gemma's abdomen and found the pelvic anatomy so distorted they couldn't find her bladder and they could see that her left fallopian tube and ovary had been pulled across the uterus to lie on the opposite side.

'It has turned a full one eighty degrees,' Ella said. 'It's extraordinary.'

'A slight rotation of the uterus is common in pregnancy.' Logan had raised his voice to include the whole team. 'It rarely exceeds forty-five degrees and it happens most often to the right. It's associated with foetal compromise and significant maternal morbidity so we need to get this baby out stat. We can't correct the torsion in a gravid uterus so we'll have to go in posteriorly. Scalpel, thanks...'

The baby girl came out completely limp and it was Ella who handed her over to the neonatal paediatric team. It was Ella who delivered the placenta by controlled cord traction under Logan's supervision and then closed the uterus in two layers. The baby's Apgar score had picked up by then and she was taken away to the NICU.

With Logan's calm instructions that were quiet enough to be just for her to hear, Ella then turned the uterus back to its correct anatomical position. Together they checked that everything in Gemma's abdomen—including the bladder that was now visible—was not a cause for concern and then it was time to close up.

'I can do this if you want to get away,' Logan offered. 'It is your day off, after all.'

'I'll see this through,' Ella responded. 'It's a once-in-a-lifetime case and I was there right from the start of it. I think this qualifies as a bit of an adventure so I don't want to miss anything.'

The closure of the abdominal wound was

routine. So routine that Ella could let her thoughts wander a little as she watched Logan's deft suturing.

Why had Logan told her about her locum position becoming available as a permanent job? Did he want her to apply for it?

Maybe he did. Because they worked so well together? His work was, after all, the most important thing in his life. Something that he had no intention of being distracted from.

But if she stayed would their personal relationship continue? Would Ella want it to when she knew she was falling more and more in love with Logan? That could end up being even more heartbreaking than leaving him to go and be almost literally a world away from him.

There was an ache somewhere below Ella's ribs that she hadn't felt for so long it took a moment or two to realise what it was. It made her remember the time when she was far away from home and got the news that her mother was so ill.

It was grief, wasn't it? The kind of grief that could start even before you were actually missing having a particular person in your life. Because you knew with every fibre of your being just how much of a hole they were going to leave in your life when they were gone.

Ella couldn't possibly stay here permanently. Because that hole might become big enough to swallow her up completely.

She put a dressing in place over the wound in Gemma's belly. 'You know what? I might go and see how the baby's doing in NICU.'

And Logan nodded but he was turning away to look at the monitor screens as Gemma was being brought out from under the general anaesthetic and Ella could feel distance being deliberately created between them. Because she'd mentioned the NICU? She'd never discovered why it was not one of his favourite places because she had respected his privacy, but feeling that distance—that barrier—was another warning that she'd got herself in too deep this time.

And it was another reason she could never stay.

Ella spent more time in NICU than she had intended but it was so good to see how well Gemma's baby daughter was doing and to hear that Gemma's husband had been contacted and was on his way to be with his wife and new baby. And then, of course, it would have been unthinkable to leave without seeing Finlay and she found Iona there in a wheelchair, having skin-to-skin time with her son, tears of joy streaming down her face.

That joy was still with Ella after she'd been to the locker rooms and changed out of her scrubs and back into civvies. She hadn't seen Logan since she'd left the theatre suite and she wasn't sure she even wanted to see him this evening, given the fear of how deeply involved she had somehow let herself get. She did, however, see someone who looked familiar as she was walking through the hospital foyer.

A pregnant woman who was holding hands with a man. And they both looked pale. Frightened…?

Ella stopped as they got closer. 'It's Margaret, isn't it? Didn't I see you at antenatal clinic last week?'

The woman nodded. 'This is my husband, Tom.'

The couple had stopped as well. They were an island of three people in the middle of a still-busy foyer, but instinct told Ella that help was needed here.

'Is everything okay?' she asked. 'Can I help?'

Margaret's eyes filled with tears. 'I can't feel my baby moving.'

Ella caught her breath. 'How long since you felt anything?'

'A couple of hours.' It was Tom who answered, as he put his arm around his wife's shoulders. 'She rang me at work when she started getting worried. I came home after that and I didn't know what to do, so I've brought her here.'

'You've done exactly the right thing,' Ella told him. 'Come with me.'

She was holding her breath as she pushed the lift button to take them to the radiology department where she knew an ultrasound room would be available.

'I looked it up online,' Margaret told Ella as she climbed onto the bed in the dim room. 'I'm thirty-seven weeks now so I know there's less room in there and there won't be so much kicking or anything. And I'd been busy doing some housework so I thought I might have missed feeling any movements and that was when I was going to start counting.'

'When was the last time you can definitely remember feeling anything?' Ella helped

Margaret pull the waistband of her skirt down to expose her well-rounded belly and tucked a paper towel in to prevent gel getting onto the clothing.

'At lunchtime. I had started to think he'd been asleep for a long time so I had something sugary. And I patted my tummy to try and wake him up and I did feel something then, but that's...' Margaret caught tears with her fingertips. 'That's hours ago...'

Ella was scanning already. She could see the outline of the baby's head and body. She could see limbs that were completely still. She changed the direction of the transducer and did a slow sweep across the lower abdomen. And then she stopped. She stared at the screen for a long, long moment, desperately wishing she didn't have to tell these parents what she could see. But she did.

'I can see the whole of baby's heart,' she told them quietly. 'And it's not moving. I'm so, so sorry but...your baby has died.'

CHAPTER TEN

LOGAN WALSH HESITATED before he was close enough to knock on the door of a very private delivery room.

He needed to gather the strength he knew he had to deal with this most difficult situation and it required a mental tightrope that allowed him the distance he needed to protect himself and the compassion that was naturally there as a doctor, as a head of department. As a fellow human being. Logan had learned long ago how to do this, but it was so much harder this time.

Because Ella was part of this.

And he knew that she hadn't hesitated to involve herself emotionally in this case and share the grief of a mother who had already lost her baby but still had to go through the birthing process.

He'd been there for a meeting with Margaret and Tom when they'd had time to process the devastating news of their baby's death. He'd talked them through the options, including waiting to go into a natural labour, which could take up to three weeks, and Margaret had chosen to be induced before being allowed to go home and prepare for the labour and birth that might not start for another forty-eight hours.

'*We'll do whatever we can to help you through this,*' Logan had promised. '*I'll come and see you as soon as you're admitted and make sure you're getting everything you need.*'

So, here he was. He knew that Margaret and Tom were in this room, along with Judy as midwife and Ella, who had promised she would be with Margaret throughout her labour. Again, Logan had seen the way Ella could connect with people so easily and he could see the bond that was already there. He also knew that Ella would be the best person that these grieving parents could have with them at this time. He probably wasn't even needed here.

He hadn't been needed by Ella in the last couple of days either. He'd tried to see her. She hadn't answered his knock on her door the night before last, and when he'd turned up last night with a takeaway meal she'd thanked him with a smile that was heartbreaking but said she wasn't hungry and that she needed to be on her own right now.

Logan understood that better than anybody and he respected Ella enough not to push into the space she wanted—or needed—to deal with alone.

But he'd promised Margaret that he would come to see her and he wasn't about to break that promise. Logan tapped lightly on the door and slipped into the room.

A lot of effort had clearly gone into the planning and preparation for this time. Margaret had her own linen and a soft woollen blanket on the bed. There were aromatherapy candles burning and soft soulful music playing in the background. Margaret was standing beside the bed, leaning forward with her hands clutching the blanket and Tom was standing beside her, rubbing her lower back. Judy was quietly in the background, like the music, but Ella was in the thick of it, leaning over the other side of the bed, her hands on top of Margaret's, her focus completely on her patient.

'Keep going, Margaret. Faster, lighter breathing as your contraction peaks—that's it… Now you can slow it down again. That's brilliant…'

Logan waited until the contraction had passed and Margaret straightened to lean back against Tom. She noticed him standing near the door.

'I won't disturb you,' Logan said. 'Is there anything else you need? Are things okay with your pain relief?' He glanced at Ella. 'Is there still time for an epidural?'

'I don't want one,' Margaret said. 'I need to feel this.'

'We've got a Luer in,' Ella said. 'We can give as much pain relief as Margaret wants.'

'You know what I really want?'

'What's that?'

'I didn't ask… I wasn't really thinking of it as the birth I planned and I didn't think it would be possible but… I really wanted to have a water birth for Tayla…'

Oh… *God*… Hearing the name of the baby was almost Logan's undoing. He could feel his protective casing cracking. It wasn't helping that he'd never seen Ella looking so sombre. Her eyes were so dark they looked black and there was a stillness to her features that was a complete contrast to the way he had become so used to seeing emotions play out on her face.

He felt a bit lost, not being able to read how Ella was feeling as easily as he'd been able to before, but maybe this was an occasion when she needed to tap into some professional distance herself, even if it was only to gather her own strength at times?

She sounded completely in control. 'We can do that for you, Margaret. I think it's a great idea.'

Judy was already turning on the taps for the birthing pool in the room. As Margaret groaned with another contraction starting, Logan caught sight of what was to one side of this space—a Moses basket with tiny clothes folded into a pile on top of the mattress. Would Ella still be here when the birth was over and the baby was gently cleaned and dressed to be given to the parents to be with for as long as they needed?

Logan was quite sure she would be.

He could be too, if it would help Ella. She didn't need to know how hard it would be for him. But when she saw the silent question in his eyes she gave a tiny shake of her head.

A hint of a smile even, to let him know that she was fine.

That she didn't need him.

The sadness stayed with Ella for days.

She would never forget delivering that perfect baby girl who had suffocated in the womb because the umbilical cord had wrapped itself around her neck, or the courage of her parents as they both welcomed and prepared to say goodbye to an already much-loved infant. It had to be one of the most profound silences you could ever hear in that space of time after the birth, when no baby's cry was going to be heard.

Margaret and Tom were left in privacy with their baby for much of the next twelve or so hours that they chose to spend with Tayla, but Ella had made herself available at all times and paid brief visits to check on how they were doing. Precious memories were being collected. A lock of hair, prints of tiny hands and feet. Visits from other family members including Tayla's big brother, Lachlan There were some hauntingly beautiful photographs taken by a studio that was experienced in handling a session like this with compassion and sensitivity.

Logan was being very sensitive as well. Ella knew there was an open invitation to talk to him or share a meal after work but she found herself pulling back. Because she knew she would probably fall apart in his arms and might even confess how she felt about him, and that would change everything. Any remaining time in her locum position here might become unbearable. And it had been her idea right from the start to make the most of the time they could be together, hadn't it? It would be a bit unfair to ruin it for both of them. She just needed a day or two to pull herself together and find the kind of optimism that had always kept her moving forward and making her life as good as it could possibly be.

She was trying to remind herself of what she'd told Logan. That protecting yourself from not feeling the pain of a distressing case meant missing out on feeling the joy of the best cases, but this was hard enough to make her wonder if Logan actually had the right idea. That the way to protect yourself and be the best doctor you could be was to keep a professional distance.

Maybe she could adjust her balance and

learn to not let her emotional pendulum swing quite so far.

She was going to give it a go. Starting from now…

Mind you, even Logan looked as though this case had got to him, despite his ability to keep that distance. He'd looked kind of tired at work over the last couple of days. A bit paler than normal, even? Perhaps it wasn't as easy as he'd made it look up till now to maintain a purely professional relationship in some cases?

Ella finished the sketches she'd made of her ideas for converting Logan's barn and put them in an envelope to leave quietly by his door before she headed out for a walk on her next day off. He must have heard her door closing or something, however, because his door opened.

'Hey…you've got a day off too?'

'Yeah… I'm just heading out for a walk. I was just leaving this for you. They're the sketches I've been doing for the barn.'

Logan slipped them out of the envelope and scanned them in silence.

'These are amazing,' he said. 'I can't thank you enough.' He caught her gaze. 'You're very talented. You know that, don't you?'

Ella shrugged. She could feel another question beneath that one.

Are you okay? Is there anything I can do to help...?

She wanted to ask the same thing of him, but it felt as if she could be treading on an emotional minefield and what she really needed was a break.

So Ella gave her head a tiny shake as a response to both Logan's questions, spoken and silent. 'You could take a photo of your favourite sketches,' she said brightly. 'And send them to your estate agent. Have you put the property on the market yet?'

'I'm about to go out there and cut the grass. I've been to the hire place this morning and got all the gear I need in my car. I just came back for a bite of lunch.' Logan's eyebrows rose. 'Would you like to come out with me? Get some fresh air?' His smile was completely crooked. 'I seem to remember you wanted some experience with grass cutting machinery to put on your CV?'

That made Ella smile, and just the act of smiling somehow made things a little bit better.

'That's true. I did say that.'

Ella could remember what Logan had said

too. About the way he'd promised to make it worth her while in that raspy, sexy voice. And maybe that was exactly what was needed here. A reset? Getting back to where they'd been, content with making the most of a temporary relationship.

'And I meant it,' Ella added. She smiled at Logan. 'Just give me a minute to put on some old clothes?'

'Take your time. I'm going to have another look at these amazing drawings of yours.'

This was just what the doctor ordered as far as Ella was concerned.

Some hard physical work outside. A world away from work and such a painful reminder of the downside of being emotionally involved with her patients. Logan seemed to sense that she didn't want to talk about anything work-related so he only talked about what they were doing. How short the grass needed to be. What branches needed to be pruned off the trees and did the ivy on the pixie house need to be trimmed?

'Yes,' Ella decreed, her arms full of pruned branches from the willow tree that she was taking to the heap, out of sight around the corner of the barn. 'But try not to cut that daisy bush that's growing near the door. That's really pretty.'

The sun came out and gave them a hint of what this garden—when it became a garden and not just an overgrown patch of meadow—would be like in summer. Both Logan and Ella took off their warm layers of clothing and got their arms scratched by branches and prickles in the grass that needed to be trimmed and raked before the mower could be used to make it look something like a lawn. They got hot and dirty and tired but it was one of the best afternoons Ella had had in a very long time.

'I think we're done,' Logan finally declared.

'Thank goodness.' Ella sat on the bank beside the pond and then dropped backwards to lie flat, closing her eyes from the low angle of the sun in the late afternoon and stretching her arms out sideways. She knew Logan had sat down beside her because his leg brushed her fingertips. He didn't say anything and as the seconds ticked by and she breathed in the delicious smell of freshly cut grass she began to hear the faint birdsong from the hedgerows and the sound of sheep in the distance. A bee buzzed overhead and something splashed in the pond. And then she heard something unexpected. An insistent peeping sound that was loud enough to make her sit up.

'Is that…?'

'It's your duck.' Logan nodded. 'Look…'

Ella shaded her eyes. The lovely big white duck with the yellow beak was swimming towards them on the pond, and behind her was a string of fluffy yellow ducklings. They came closer and closer and then climbed out of the pond to inspect the newly mown grass.

'Oh…*oh*…' Ella found her eyes suddenly filling with tears. 'They're so adorable…' She swiped a tear away. 'This is exactly what I needed after such a horrible week at work. Thank you, Logan.' She turned to smile at him, wanting to kiss him perhaps, but as soon as she saw his face she froze.

She wasn't the only one crying.

Logan was staring at the ducklings. And he had tears rolling down the side of his nose.

And Ella's heart was breaking.

'What is it?' she asked softly. 'What's wrong?'

She could see the effort that Logan was making to control himself. To push things away. Whatever it was, he didn't want to talk about it, but this time Ella wasn't going to let him run away. She wanted to understand. There was something hurting the man she loved and she desperately needed to know what it was.

'Tell me,' she whispered. 'Does it have something to do with Tayla?'

Logan closed his eyes. 'I met them,' he said, his voice catching. 'Margaret and Tom. When they were leaving the hospital. They were taking Tayla to the funeral home themselves and they had her in that Moses basket. Anyone who'd seen her would have thought she was just a perfect sleeping baby but...'

'...but you knew,' Ella finished for him. 'And it broke your heart.' She reached for his hand and held it.

'She looked so like another baby I knew,' Logan said, and it was the pain in his voice that made Ella guess what he wasn't saying.

'*Your* baby? Oh, my God, Logan... Did you lose a baby?'

He was silent for such a long time that Ella thought he wasn't going to answer her, but then he nodded. He opened his eyes but he was still looking in front of him, at where the ducklings were pecking the ground, searching for bugs.

'I'd just graduated from medical school

and was about to start my first Foundation Year,' he said slowly. 'Katie and I had been married for a couple of years by then and we were expecting our first baby in a few weeks. We were moving into a new flat and she suddenly got terrible abdominal pain. And she was bleeding. I called an ambulance and went into Emergency with her, but everything took far too long and I didn't know enough to realise how much trouble Katie was in. All I could do was trust the people involved and I'd never felt so helpless in my life. By the time they got to Theatre and found she'd had a uterine rupture it was too late. She'd lost too much blood. She arrested in Theatre and they couldn't get her back.'

Ella swallowed the painful lump in her throat. So this was why Logan had made it his mission in life to train people to recognise obstetric emergencies early enough to make it more likely that lives could be saved. It also explained why he considered himself 'married' to his work. He'd gone through the agony of losing the woman he'd loved enough to marry and it was easy to understand why he never wanted to risk his heart like that again.

But it was so sad... Logan had so much

love, so much tenderness that he *could* give if he could bring himself to take that risk. And he could get it back and…and find that special kind of joy in life.

Logan cleared his throat. 'Our baby—Sam—survived the surgery, but only just. He'd been without oxygen for too long and we knew he wasn't going to survive, but somehow he held on. For weeks. I was given special leave and I sat with him in NICU every day for hours and hours. I got to hold him.' There were tears on Logan's face again. 'Until I couldn't. Until the day I buried him in Katie's arms.'

Ella had tears on her own cheeks. The final pieces of the puzzle were coming together and she now knew exactly why the NICU was not one of Logan's favourite places. She could imagine him sitting there beside an incubator with a tiny, fragile infant struggling to survive. A struggle that had been tragically lost after a valiant fight lasting so long when even a day would feel like a week. And she remembered that day when she'd been sitting beside Finlay in the NICU and the baby boy had opened his eyes and looked at her and she had been so sure he was going to make it that she couldn't help shedding a happy tear or two. And she'd looked up to see Logan watching her through the window and thought he was clearly disapproving of her involvement in that case.

But how badly had he been hurting in that moment?

Logan Walsh had buried his son in his wife's arms. It couldn't be any more tragic than that. Ella could understand completely that any desire to be that involved with anyone ever again had been buried along with them.

She had no words to tell him how her own heart was breaking on his behalf, but she moved so that she was on her knees beside Logan and she put her arms around him. He buried his face against her shoulder and neck and she bent her head to touch his. She could hold him for as long as he wanted.

And they could cry together. Because Ella suspected that it might have been far too long since Logan had let himself feel this grief at all, let alone to share it with someone else.

You never knew. This might be what he remembered about her for the rest of his life and it was a gift she was only too happy to give. Because she knew now, beyond a shadow of doubt, that she was totally and utterly in love with Logan.

And what she really wanted to give were the words that were scrambling to get out of her head—and her heart.

She desperately wanted to tell him that he was loved. That *she* loved him. As much as it was possible to love another human being. Enough to want to spend the rest of her life with him.

But how could she?

Especially knowing what she now knew about him. That he'd not only lost the woman he'd loved but his baby son as well. She knew how much love he was capable of giving because she had been able to feel the edges of it from the very first time he'd made love to her, so she knew just how devastating that must have been. That Logan might never want to risk living through that kind of pain again.

She also couldn't tell him because she knew he cared about her enough to not want to hurt her and, if he knew how she felt, he might be unable to stop himself responding by saying he loved her back. Asking her to stay for more reasons than to simply fill a consultant vacancy on his staff. To offer her something that he might think was genuine even, but if it wasn't offered freely—without any kind of pressure—she would never know if it was real. To offer herself and potentially give up the freedom that had been the best part of her life for so many years now could turn out to be a soul-destroying mistake that she might never recover from.

So Ella held in those words as tightly as she was holding Logan.

Both physical and emotional weariness wrapped them both in a sombre silence as they travelled back to the city a while later. They both knew that something huge had changed between them and it seemed that neither of them wanted to talk about it.

Because they both knew it marked the end of the road?

They'd both known that what they had was supposed to be temporary, but Ella was feeling more miserable than ever now. Because it wasn't supposed to end quite this soon.

CHAPTER ELEVEN

By TACIT AGREEMENT, both Ella and Logan gave each other space over the next couple of weeks, perhaps because they were both waiting for any sign that the other was wanting something closer than being friendly colleagues. Or maybe it was because they had got too close the day of the grass cutting and it was instinctive to retreat to a safer place.

Ella hated it to begin with but she soon realised how helpful it was in her new mission to learn how to keep a safe emotional distance. She focused on her work, on keeping a smile on her face and a cheerful rapport with her patients as she reassured them in antenatal clinics, supported them through any investigations or interventions they needed and shared the challenge and triumph of bringing their babies into the world.

She was happy to let Logan retreat into

his own space because she recognised that he might need to do that for his own peace of mind. His own dignity, even? And she suspected early on that maybe he was doing his best to avoid meeting her in the hallways of the doctors' residence in the same way she was avoiding him—by listening for the sound of his door closing and then waiting long enough for the coast to be clear before she went out of her apartment.

When they did see each other, on the way to or from work and when they were working together, they were ultimately professional. And friendly. And, okay…if they made eye contact with each other, there was always a frisson of just how well they knew each other but also an agreement that it was over. Ella wondered if it was like this now because they knew each other *too* well. That perhaps Logan was quite well aware of how she felt about him and he was trying to be kind in escaping something he didn't want in his life.

He had the right to be alone if that was his choice and Ella couldn't hold it against him. He'd made it perfectly clear from the start that he didn't want a significant relationship. He hadn't even wanted anyone 'hitting on him'. That private joke had a very poignant note to it now, which meant it was probably already being consigned to being no more than a memory that would resurface every time she heard the phrase in the future. Like remembering that Logan had seen her doing her stupid happy dance in the hospital corridor if she ever felt like dancing again. Or the significance that zebras versus horses would always have whenever she was listing differential diagnoses for any medical challenge.

As she neared the end of the second week of being simply colleagues again, Ella knocked on the door of Logan's office.

'Have you got a minute?'

'For you? Of course.' Logan closed the lid of the laptop he was working on. 'What's up?'

'I wondered whether you've had applicants for the consultant position here yet?'

There was a flash in Logan's eyes that Ella couldn't interpret. Did he think she'd changed her mind about applying for the job? Was he hoping that she wouldn't?

'A few,' he said cautiously. 'Why?'

'How soon do you think you could appoint someone?'

'Ah…that would depend on a few factors. Like whether they needed to give notice from their current position or shift from another city or country, even.' Logan was frowning now. 'Why do you ask?'

'I've been contacted by the hospital in Australia that I'm heading for next. They're desperate to fill their gap and have asked me if there's any possibility of getting there a bit earlier than planned. I don't want to leave you in the lurch but...' Ella's gaze slid away from Logan's. 'It feels like it might be a good time to move on...'

The silence grew in the small room until it started to feel awkward. And then Logan cleared his throat.

'I'll see what I can do,' he said. 'And I understand. Moving on is a good thing. I've got an offer on the barn that's just come in.'

He was smiling as Ella lifted her gaze in surprise. That crooked smile that caught her heart like a hook, every time. More now, in fact, because she could feel the undercurrents for Logan. Everything that had happened to make him the man he was today. How much his smiles actually meant.

'The estate agent told me it was your sketches that sealed the deal.' Was there a tone of forced brightness in Logan's voice? 'The buyers could apparently see themselves on a summer evening, outside on that courtyard, having a barbecue. Or sitting in the pixie house, watching the ducks on the pond.'

Oh…that would be a dream of her own for ever, Ella realised. It would be…home, that was what it would be. But only if Logan was there.

'Are you going to accept the offer?'

'It's a good offer. I'd be silly not to accept it. I've got the contract right here. I just need to sign it and send it back.'

Ella nodded, swallowing hard at the same time. She excused herself then, desperately needing to escape Logan's office and try and walk away from the idea of other people doing the barn conversion she had put her heart and soul into creating. Even worse was the thought of other people in that pixie house where Logan had very nearly kissed her for the first time.

In the rain.

It had been raining that first day when she'd got soaked walking to her new accommodation and found herself locked out.

It was raining again today. More than raining, in fact. It might be well into spring in Scotland but there was snow mixed in with that relentless rain. It was sleeting and freezing and about as miserable outside as Ella was feeling at the thought of Logan walking away from the barn or that she could be packing up to move to the other side of the world in a matter of days.

Ella wasn't in any hurry to get home. Because it didn't feel like home any longer? It was just an apartment. Temporary lodging. For a place to feel like a home it needed to be somewhere she wanted to be. Or with someone she wanted to be with?

Logan's barn felt like a home. Even though it was completely uninhabitable at the moment.

It was going to get dark early, though, thanks to this horrible weather so as soon as Ella noticed a break in the precipitation she headed for the locker room to change out of her scrubs. She'd known it would be cold and miserable today, so she'd come to work wearing jeans tucked into her boots and a tee shirt beneath her favourite alpaca jumper. She was reaching for her anorak when Logan burst into the room. He headed straight for his locker.

'There's a call-out,' he told Ella. 'For OERT.'

'Oh, no… In this weather?'

'It's because of the weather that the call's been made.' Logan stripped off the tunic of his scrub suit and Ella found herself staring at his naked back as he kept talking. 'Do you remember that B&B we passed up on the Old Military Road, when we were coming back from Inverness?'

'Yes...' Suddenly it was easy to focus on what Logan was saying and not what she was watching as he pulled a tee shirt over his head and then reached for the dark fisherman's rib jumper hanging on the hook inside his locker. 'Is that where you're going?'

'Aye. There's a woman alone in the house. And she's been in labour for hours now.' Logan pulled the jumper on. 'Her midwife can't get to her. The helicopter can't go up in this weather. We can't even send an ambulance because they don't have chains and it's already snowing heavily and beginning to settle.'

'Is she at risk of complications?' Ella was already imagining how frightened the mother would be. She barely noticed that Logan was taking off the trousers of his scrub suit to pull on a pair of chinos. 'Is it her first baby?'

'It's not only her first baby, she lost her husband just before she knew she was pregnant. Her midwife said that this pregnancy has been the only thing that's kept her going.' Logan took his shoes and socks to the bench that ran down the centre of the room and sat down to put them on. 'She hasn't got any known risk factors but…'

He lifted his gaze to catch Ella's and there was far more than a frisson of intimacy there. She understood instantly why he wasn't going to let this woman deliver a baby alone when her whole future might depend on the outcome.

'I'm going to take my SUV,' Logan said. 'I've got a set of chains so it should be fine as long as I head off ASAP. I've got the usual OERT gear good to go. He held the gaze a heartbeat longer. 'Will you come with me?' he asked quietly. 'I think we make a team where the sum is greater than the parts.'

A part of Ella's heart was melting at those quiet words. She understood exactly what Logan meant because she knew she was a better doctor when he was by her side. She was more confident. More courageous. Just… more of everything she wanted to be in her life, really. She just hadn't imagined that Logan might feel the same way.

'Of course I will,' she said.

* * *

They barely spoke on the drive.

Logan was completely focused on the road conditions and the deteriorating weather. Ella was almost hypnotised by the swirl of snowflakes rushing towards them in the muted glare of the vehicle's headlights. The road was white by the time they got to the high altitude of the mountain pass but the rugged tyres of the SUV were able to cope and they didn't need to stop to put the chains on.

'We're going to be stuck up here overnight at least,' Logan warned. 'But the forecast for tomorrow is much better. They're saying this low pressure will be short but sharp. I'm sure they'll be able to clear the road in daylight.'

'I'm not bothered,' Ella told him. 'I just hope we get there in time.'

They arrived in plenty of time. The mother, Maureen, was already worn out by the hours of painful contractions and terrified of giving birth alone and she was so happy to see Logan and Ella arrive that she burst into floods of tears and, dammit, but Ella was crying already too.

Just a bit. A single tear that she swiped away very fast and Maureen didn't seem to notice. If Logan had noticed he didn't seem to mind, but then he was looking a lot less calm and controlled than usual himself.

'It's a wee bit bleak out there,' he told Maureen after they'd introduced themselves properly and it was obvious that a birth was not imminent. 'But we're here and we're not going anywhere any time soon. How 'bout I get your fire going and get the rest of our gear inside while Ella has a look to see what's going on for you?'

The back of Logan's car had been stacked with all sorts of equipment. They had a portable CTG machine, a portable ultrasound machine, a cylinder of Entonox as one form of pain relief, along with a raft of drugs and IV supplies. They also had a kit for assisted delivery with forceps and a disposal ventouse suction cup and pump.

'You've done a brilliant job so far,' Ella told Maureen. 'You're about six centimetres dilated already and baby's doing well. I'm more than happy with the heart rate and the response to your contractions. Let's see how comfortable we can get you before you transition into second stage of labour. Would you like a nice warm shower or bath and then we can find something really comfortable for you to wear?'

'I'd like that,' Maureen said. 'I've got a cotton knit nightdress in my hospital bag. It's in the bedroom upstairs.' Then she bit her lip. 'I don't want to go up there to have my baby, though… I'd rather do it here.'

'I could bring the mattress from your bed down here into the living room,' Logan offered. 'It's lovely and warm in here now with the fire going and you may want to deliver lying down.'

'We'll pop a line in your hand too,' Ella said. 'After you've had your shower. That way we'll be able to give you some stronger pain relief if you need it.'

'It's a boy,' Maureen told them when Ella slipped a cannula into a vein on the back of her hand a while later and secured it with tape. 'I'm going to call him Dougal…after his dadda.' She pressed her other hand against her mouth to stifle a sob. 'I'm sorry… It's just been so hard to be doing this without him. I miss him *so* much…'

'I know you do.' It was Logan who put his hand over Maureen's. 'And I'm so sorry for your loss. He'd be very proud of you right now.'

Maureen was smiling through her tears. 'Do you really think so?'

'Absolutely I do.'

Logan's smile was gentle. He was still holding Maureen's hand as her next contraction started and Ella watched in amazement as she saw lines on Logan's face that looked as though he was actually feeling some of the pain Maureen was in. He was emotionally connected, she realised. He didn't seem to have any of the professional distance she'd come to expect of this doctor. What had made the change? Tapping into his own traumatic past?

And would that mean the calm confidence he displayed in coping with any problems would be inaccessible?

In the next hour they kept a close watch on the baby's heart rate during contractions and helped Maureen change position and walk around a little. They gave her sips of water and had snacks available, although they weren't wanted. As the end of her first stage of labour approached, Maureen got a little anxious.

'What time is it?' she asked.

'Nearly eleven p.m.'

'Is it still snowing?'

'It looks like a Christmas card outside.'

'Oh, no… You're not going to be able to get home after this.'

'We weren't planning to go anywhere until it's clear enough to get transport for you to get to hospital.'

Maureen nodded, pushing her hair back from her face. 'It's no worry. The bedroom we use for guests is always made up with clean sheets. It's out in the barn so it might be far too cold, though. But there's a spare bedroom upstairs, next to ours, and it's always warm when the fire's going because the chimney's part of the wall.' She was pacing now, bent over and rubbing her own back.

'This was our dream, you know… To be on the family farm but run a B&B as well and share the countryside that we both loved. We wanted a whole bunch of bairns to be running around out there…'

She walked towards the fireplace and then stopped. 'It was so sudden,' she told them. 'Dougal got sick and we found out he had pancreatic cancer and…and he died only six weeks later. He didn't even know he was going to be a daddy.' Maureen's face twisted into lines of renewed pain, both emotional and physical. When she cried out with an agonised groan, Logan and Ella both helped her back to the mattress, where she crumpled and knelt down to ride out what seemed to be a noticeably longer and stronger contraction than any earlier ones.

'You're fully dilated,' Ella was able to confirm moments later. 'It's time to start pushing. I think we're going to be meeting wee Dougal soon.'

Except they didn't. Fifteen minutes of regular contractions and hard pushing from Maureen turned into thirty minutes.

Thirty minutes became an hour and then an hour and a half. Maureen was exhausted and Logan and Ella began exchanging concerned glances. When they began to see changes in the baby's heart rate during contractions, Logan crouched beside Maureen, who was on all fours.

'I can see his head, Maureen. You're almost there. Big push...'

'Keep it going,' Ella encouraged when the next contraction started. 'Keep pushing. Push, push...push.'

Maureen had her head bowed and her groan sounded desperate. 'I can't do this... It's too hard...'

The baby's head hadn't moved during the last contraction.

'I need to examine you,' Logan said. 'And see what's going on. I'm sorry, it won't be very comfortable.'

Ella held her breath. She watched Logan's face as he gave her an internal examination and she saw the moment he realised what was going on.

'Your baby's shoulders are a wee bit stuck,' he told Maureen. 'He's going to need some help to come out. Stay where you are for the moment. I'm going to need to give you an episiotomy to make a bit more room. Are you okay with that?'

Maureen nodded. She sounded frightened now. 'Just help…please…get my baby out safely…'

Logan's gaze met Ella's as he looked up to take the syringe of local anaesthetic she had drawn up and then the sterile scissors from the pack she'd opened to hold out for him.

Shoulder dystocia. The baby's head was delivered but his shoulders were stuck inside the pelvis. They had only a few minutes to get him out before there was a significant risk to the baby.

'My hands are smaller than yours,' Ella said quietly. 'Shall I try a Rubin's manoeuvre?'

Logan nodded. 'Let's get you lying down on the mattress,' he told Maureen. 'You're going to feel Ella trying to rotate the baby a little to help his shoulders come out.'

Ella slipped her hand in to find the posterior shoulder of the baby to rotate it to an oblique position.

'Can you give me some suprapubic pressure, please, Logan?'

'I need to push,' Maureen gasped.

'Not yet.' Logan sounded just as calm as he always had in any emergency situation Ella had shared with him. 'Just wait, Maureen. You'll be able to push as soon as we get a shoulder free.'

Ella was still trying to get her fingers into the right position to push the underneath shoulder around. Logan was waiting to help by pressing on the upper shoulder. They both knew that if this failed they'd have to work very fast with another manoeuvre and if *that* didn't work they might have to break the baby's clavicle. Ella really, really didn't want to have to do that, but if that was what it took to save Maureen's baby, of course she would do it.

But…this was working. She could feel the baby rotating under her hand, with the shoulder moving away from her fingers and his face turning upwards into her other hand. She cupped the chin with that hand and the back of his head with her other hand and helped him rotate further, easing first one shoulder and then the other through the pelvis.

'You can push now, Maureen,' she said. 'He's coming….and…here he is.' Ella lifted the newborn and, to her enormous relief, he was already taking his first breath and getting ready to give his first cry, which startled them all with how loud it was.

'Good set of lungs.' Logan was grinning.

'Oh…*oh…*' Maureen was trying to sit up, reaching for her baby.

Logan helped. With the umbilical cord still attached, he got the baby settled against his mother's chest, skin to skin, with pillows supporting her and a warm blanket over them both.

And then, after the maelstrom of extreme tension and pain and effort and the relief of the baby arriving safely, there was suddenly a silence in this room.

Baby Dougal was lying on his mother's bare skin, looking up at her, and he was completely silent. Ella was simply soaking in the joy of the moment before starting to think about the third stage of labour and watching for anything of concern like excessive post-partum bleeding. Logan seemed equally stunned. He still had his hand on the pillows behind Maureen that he'd been adjusting but he stopped moving.

It felt as if they were all holding their breath and the only sound was the soft crackle of the fire that was warming this room so well and creating soft flickers of light.

It was Maureen who broke the silence.

'He's so perfect,' she whispered. 'Welcome to the world, Dougal…' She lifted her gaze then, staring at the doorway of the room that led to the stairs. 'He's here,' she said softly. 'Your dadda, Dougal. I can feel that he's here.'

'He is…' Ella's tears were really falling this time. 'He'll always be here. In your home and in your heart. And wee Dougal will grow up knowing who he is because of how much you loved his dadda. How much you loved each other…'

She looked up to catch Logan's gaze when she finished speaking and it felt like she'd just told him how much she loved *him*. To her amazement, his gaze held hers with a softness that suggested he understood and it wasn't something he was about to run away from.

It almost felt like he wanted to echo her own words.

It was in the early hours of the morning by the time Maureen had finished her labour and was tucked up into her warm makeshift bed with Dougal beside her in a Moses basket, so close that she could press a featherlight kiss to the whorls of hair on her baby's head before snuggling beneath the feather duvet Logan had brought downstairs.

'Try and sleep,' he suggested. 'Goodness knows you deserve a rest.'

'I can't tell you how happy I am you were here with me.' Maureen lay back on her pillows, her eyes drifting closed. 'I can't believe how happy *I* am, to be honest.' She opened her eyes again, looking straight at Logan. 'Do you know, I hated it when I knew I was pregnant. I thought I couldn't do this without Dougal. I wanted to just curl up and hide from the world for ever.'

Her words were gripping Logan's heart so hard it was difficult to take a breath. He'd never let himself become this emotionally involved with a patient but there was no way he could have prevented it this time. He wouldn't have wanted to.

'I know,' he said softly. And he did. He knew how that felt. It was his work that had forced him to keep going. Maureen's pregnancy must have become the same kind of escape from the depths of grief.

'This is a new life for me,' Maureen whispered. 'And it's going to be wonderful. I have someone to love again.' She reached out to touch baby Dougal's head with her fingertips and she might have been talking to him rather than Logan. 'You've got to take the risk of loving someone this much again.' Her words were fading now. Maybe she was just thinking aloud. 'Otherwise you're not really living at all...'

Within seconds, Maureen was as soundly asleep as her baby.

'I don't know about you,' Ella said. 'But I'm desperate for a cup of tea. Maybe something to eat too. I'm sure Maureen won't mind if I poke around in her kitchen for a bit.'

He watched Ella go through the open archway that led to a big kitchen dining room in this old farmhouse but he stayed watching Maureen and the baby, even though it was for purely emotional reasons. His pendulum really had swung far too far on this call-out but the fear that it could lead to him making bad decisions had been unfounded, hadn't it?

Maybe it was because he was isolated so far from any hospital. Or, more likely, it was because he'd been working with Ella by his side, but he felt as though he'd made *better* decisions.

And he knew that Ella had been right and he could understand why and how she connected so well with people—because there was so much more joy that could be found in the work they did if they let it touch their hearts. There was no medical reason that made it necessary for him to sit there any longer. Their patients were both doing very well. No doubt they would clear the roads in the morning and an ambulance would be able to come and take this mother and infant in for more extensive checks in hospital but, for now, all they needed to do was rest.

Logan had something he needed to do before dawn broke, however, before any part of the rest of the world intruded into this time and space he would remember for the rest of his life. He went into the kitchen.

'I've made cheese on toast,' Ella told him. 'But it's too hot to eat just yet.' She was smiling at him. 'I don't want you to burn your tongue.'

Logan couldn't smile back. 'I don't want you to go to Australia,' he said. 'I love you, Ella Grisham.'

He saw the way her eyes widened and then she became so very, very still.

'I love you too, Logan Walsh,' she whispered. 'But I do really understand why you can't go there. Why you can't risk your heart again.'

Logan took a step closer. He reached to take and hold both of Ella's hands.

'Maureen's a wise woman,' he said slowly. 'I think I already knew what she said about not really being alive unless you loved someone, but it was so much easier to ignore it. To not take that risk and just pretend that everything was fine the way it was. To not even think that there might be a zebra amongst that herd of horses going past in your life.'

How weird was it that Ella felt as if she completely understood what Logan was saying? That she was the person he wanted to be with. Because she was different. This—what they'd found together—was different. Incredibly rare.

Worth risking your heart for, because if you didn't take that risk you weren't truly living.

More than worth giving up what she had perceived as freedom for as well.

'I've been travelling for so long,' she said aloud. 'Moving from place to place and meeting so many people.'

'Because you need your freedom.' Logan nodded. 'I get that. I understand why you don't want to stay still.'

But Ella shook her head. 'I think I knew it was time to stay still the day you took me to see your barn. I think I had to do all that travelling to find you. To find the home I've been searching for.'

'I didn't sign that contract,' Logan told her. 'I couldn't. I kept thinking of you in the pixie house and your ducks and… I didn't want anyone else to be living in *our* barn.'

'*Our* barn…' Ella breathed. 'Oh… I love that idea…almost as much as I love you, Logan.'

'You mean…you'll stay?' Logan's gaze was fixed on Ella's. 'Here, in Aberdeen? Here… with me?'

Ella dropped her hands and stood on tiptoes so that she could put her arms around his neck. 'I should warn you,' she said solemnly, 'I'm hitting on you, Logan.'

The side of his mouth lifted in that quirky smile of his. 'I should warn you. It's doomed to succeed.' He was dipping his head to kiss her. 'But I think I should warn *you* because I think it's actually me that's hitting on you. Because I love you. I may well be hitting on you for as long as you'll let me. A lifetime, I hope…'

'Mutual hitting,' Ella murmured in the blink of time before his lips touched her own. 'For ever. The very best kind…'

EPILOGUE

Four years later...

ELLA'S BELOVED ALPACA jumper had a few holes in it these days, but she was still wearing it because it was unlikely she was ever going to be able to choose a replacement for it on a trip to Peru.

And she could not be happier about that.

She needed to wear it this evening because there was a hint of snow in the air and she was outside, standing beside the pond, armed with the ducks' favourite food, which was a mixture of bought duck 'crumble', vegetable peelings and suitable leftovers. Today it was green peas from last night's dinner which the expanding flock of ducks were snapping up first from the grass as Ella scattered hand-fuls of the mix.

'El...' Logan was calling from one of the French doors on this side of the barn that he'd opened just a little. 'Come into the warm, darling. The boys will be here any minute.'

'Coming...'

Ella turned back to the house with a grin. The 'boys' were turning thirty years old today and it was going to be the first time in years that they'd all been in the same place at the same time. The first time they would be seeing the home that she and Logan had so painstakingly designed for their barn conversion. It had taken a long time to get planning permission, find the right craftsmen to do the work and source every material and feature needed from architectural antiques and recycled treasures.

Logan had a roaring fire going in the stone-built fireplace and the huge dining table was set, ready for the feast both she and Logan had been preparing all day.

'We could have done takeaway, you know,' Ella had told him. 'My brothers are not the least bit fussy about what they eat. The odd horse has probably gone missing here and there because they got hungry enough.'

It just took a glance.

Or was it the mention of a horse?

Whatever. They'd not only developed a kind of telepathy over the years but they had so much shared history now. So many private jokes or significant memories. Takeaway food would always remind them both of the meal that had been stone cold thanks to the first time they'd ever made love. And neither of them could ever forget that they were each other's 'zebra'. And, like zebras, they had very different patterns in their stripes but that didn't mean that they didn't belong together.

They both knew they were perfect for each other.

Ella's triplet brothers arrived en masse, having shared the same rental car from the airport. None of them had brought anyone else with them.

'What is wrong with you all?' Ella demanded when they all had drinks in their hands and were thawing out in front of the fire. 'Where are the girlfriends? Wives, even?'

There was a shout of male laughter. It was Mick who turned the table, however. 'Where are the babies, Ella? You guys have been married for…what it is…three years now?'

'Three and a half. And the babies are all at work.' Ella looked up at Logan, who was standing right beside her, his arm around her waist. 'We're very happy the way we are, thanks. I suspect you lot put me off having babies for ever.'

Except…she and Logan had been invited to wee Dougal's fourth birthday party not so long ago and seeing Logan with the little boy had made her wonder whether he might be hiding a secret desire to have a child of his own. Because he thought it would be the last thing Ella would want?

She could feel her gaze softening into something that felt like pure love as she held Logan's gaze a heartbeat longer. She might have to let him know that it might be easy to persuade her to change her mind if it was something he wanted. As long as it wasn't triplets.

And if Logan was their daddy.

The shout of male laughter after Ella's jibe at her brothers was fading.

'And you've put us off finding girlfriends to bring home,' Jimmysaid. 'Let alone marry. You set the bar too high, Ella.'

Eddie was gazing around the huge space that was the long side of the barn. 'This was a wreck the last time I was here. Wasn't there even a cow skeleton in the corner?'

'There was,' Logan told him. 'Wow…has it been that long since you visited?'

'Australia's a long way away,' Eddie said. 'That's why I couldn't come to your wedding. Oh, wait…we didn't get invited, did we?'

There was more laughter but it was totally good-natured.

'We didn't invite anyone,' Ella said. 'You know that. We went off to the most amazing island and had a ceremony just for us in the ruins of an old church. If you ever get a chance to visit Iona, you really should.'

'There are forty-eight Scottish kings buried there,' Logan added. 'And it really is a magical place.'

'I won't get there on this visit.' Eddie-shook his head. 'I've got to get back to my uni course and exams aren't that far off.'

'Are you still working towards your critical care paramedic qualifications?' Ella asked.

'Nope. They're done and dusted. I'm getting some helicopter credentials now that'll take me anywhere I want to go.'

'Where *do* you want to go?'

'Dunno. I think I'll stay in Australasia for a while. It's beginning to feel like home.'

'And I'm thinking of taking a break,' Mick put in. 'I might go and join Médecins Sans

Frontières and see if I can do some good in the world.'

'What about you, Jimmy?' Logan asked. 'Are you happy where you are? You've just finished a surgical rotation, haven't you? How was that?'

'Loved the surgery.' James nodded. 'But now that I'm in the emergency department I think I might have found the place I'm meant to be. It just feels like what I could be happy doing for the rest of my life.'

'When you know, you know,' Logan agreed.

'Same goes for people,' Ella added. 'One of these days, you boys will find that out. You'll find your person and you'll just know. Like I did with Logan.'

'Yeah, yeah...' Mick was looking around as if he wanted to find a way to change the subject and his eyebrows were rising. 'This might be a silly question,' he said, 'but why do you guys have a picture of zebras on your wall?'

Logan and Ella shared another glance. And a smile...

'We just like them,' Ella said. She raised her glass. 'Hey... Happy Birthday again, by the way. Here's to the next thirty years and an amazing future for you all.'

'You too,' they chorused.

'We've already got ours sorted.' Ella leaned her head against Logan's arm and he bent his head to place a kiss on her hair. 'It's your turn now.'

* * * * *

If you enjoyed this story, check out these other great reads from Alison Roberts

Secret Son to Change His Life
How to Rescue the Heart Doctor
The Doctor's Christmas Homecoming
One Weekend in Prague

All available now!